THE E

This is a work of fiction. Similarities to real people, places, or events are entirely coincidental.

THE EXTRACTION

First edition. October 6, 2024.

Copyright © 2024 Brian Leslie.

ISBN: 979-8224445783

Written by Brian Leslie.

Table of Contents

INTRODUCTION 1
CHAPTER 1 5
CHAPTER 2 21
CHAPTER 3 32
CHAPTER 4 47
CHAPTER 5 59
CHAPTER 6 79
CHAPTER 7 94
CHAPTER 8 104
CHAPTER 9 122
CHAPTER 10 142
CHAPTER 11 160
CHAPTER 12 172
CHAPTER 13 184
CHAPTER 14 199
CHAPTER 15 213
CHAPTER 16 228
CHAPTER 17 245
CHAPTER 18 261
CHAPTER 19 276
CHAPTER 20 292

INTRODUCTION

The dusty streets of Baghdad lay silent in the early hours before dawn, but a covert team of elite C.O.R.E. (Covert Operations for Retrieval and Extraction) agents prepared to breach the stillness. Their mission: extract Ali-Shabaab, a high-value asset holding vital intelligence about an imminent terrorist attack targeting Tel Aviv. Under direct orders from Washington D.C., the team led by hardened operative Arthur Duggins had to navigate the hostile factions controlling the region while racing against the clock.

As they infiltrated enemy territory with silent precision, tensions simmered among the tight-knit crew over conflicting loyalties and long-buried secrets. Unbeknownst to them, the very mission had been compromised by double agents embedded within military intelligence - traitors eager to dangle Ali-Shabaab as bait to lure out rival groups hellbent on revenge against both Mossad and American forces.

Just as they secured the target amidst a blaze of gunfire, the betrayal burst into the open. Jose Beals, Duggins' trusted second-in-command, revealed his true colors - attempting to wrest control of Ali-Shabaab to sell to the highest bidder. With bullets whizzing past, Duggins faced an agonizing choice: protect the priceless informant at all costs or terminate him to prevent his capture.

The moral complexities spiraled as alliances shattered and Ali-Shabaab's true identity emerged - he was not merely an asset, but someone with deep ties to the terrorist underworld that could shift the entire balance of the escalating Israeli-Palestinian conflict.

THE EXTRACTION

In the heart-pounding firefight, a stray bullet struck the informant, mortally wounding him before he could reveal his final secrets.

Forced to abort the mission, the battered team fled into the war-torn streets carrying Ali-Shabaab's broken body and a cryptic clue about a spectacular attack looming over Tel Aviv. The path ahead promised only more bloodshed as they sought refuge, unsure of who they could trust back at headquarters.

At the emergency rendezvous point, a shocking revelation emerged - Virginia Turner, the intelligence coordinator overseeing the op, was the mastermind behind the double-cross. She desperately coveted Ali-Shabaab's information to secretly trade with a sinister third party. A vicious gunbattle erupted, leaving Turner dead but confirming the worst - the terror cell's plans were already in motion to detonate a series of coordinated vehicle bombs across Tel Aviv on a holiday celebrating peace in the region.

With the clock ticking, the surviving C.O.R.E. agents hijacked a military transport to race to Israel, hoping to leverage Ali-Shabaab's final clues to pinpoint the attack locations. In a whirlwind final act, they tear through the streets of Tel Aviv, narrowly aborting each bombing one-by-one through desperate measures. But will they find the final lynchpin to disarm the whole operation before it's too late?

As the smoke clears, Duggins and his team are left to ponder the harrowing choices that had to be made to prevent catastrophe. In this shadow world of tradecraft and shifting alliances, truth is always the final sacrifice when national security hangs in the balance. They return to an uncertain future, their bonds of trust frayed but ultimately stronger for having stared into the abyss together.

CHAPTER 1

The acrid smell of gunpowder filled Arthur's nostrils as he pressed his back against the crumbling stone wall. Bullets whizzed past, chipping away at the ancient structure that was their only cover.

"Sitrep!" Arthur barked into his comm, his voice steady despite the chaos.

"Two hostiles at your three o'clock, boss," came the terse reply from Rodriguez, their sniper perched on a nearby rooftop. "Can't get a clean shot."

Arthur's mind raced, analyzing their predicament. They were pinned down in a narrow alley, the extraction point tantalizingly close yet unreachable under the current barrage. He could feel the weight of responsibility pressing down on him, heavier than the tactical gear strapped to his body.

"Jenkins, smoke grenade. On my mark," Arthur ordered, his eyes scanning the alleyway for any advantage.

"Copy that," Jenkins responded, the tension evident in his voice.

As Arthur prepared to give the signal, a bullet struck dangerously close, showering him with debris. He flinched involuntarily, a rare crack in his usually unflappable demeanor.

'Focus, Duggins,' he chided himself internally. 'Your team is counting on you.'

"Now!" Arthur shouted, springing into action as Jenkins lobbed the smoke grenade. The alley quickly filled with thick, choking smoke.

As they made their move, Arthur's mind flickered briefly to the intel they'd recovered. Was it worth the risk? The lives of his team? He pushed the doubts aside, concentrating on the immediate threat.

"Move! Move! Move!" he commanded, leading the charge through the smokescreen, his weapon at the ready. The sound of confused shouts from their pursuers filled the air, mixing with the staccato of gunfire.

Arthur's heart pounded in his chest, adrenaline coursing through his veins as they raced toward the extraction point. He knew the danger was far from over, but for now, they had a fighting chance.

Arthur's mind raced, analyzing their options as the smoke began to thin. He caught a glimpse of a partially collapsed building to their right, its crumbling facade offering potential cover.

"Team, on me. We're going high," Arthur commanded, his voice low but firm. Without hesitation, he led them towards the structure, his keen eyes scanning for structural weaknesses.

As they approached, Arthur noticed a rusted fire escape barely clinging to the building's side. "Jenkins, grappling hook. We're making our own entrance."

Jenkins, a compact man with wiry strength, moved swiftly. "On it, boss," he replied, uncoiling the hook with practiced efficiency.

While Jenkins worked, Arthur turned to the rest of his team. "Ramirez, you're our eyes. Take position and cover our ascent."

Ramirez, a former sniper with unparalleled marksmanship, nodded silently. Her dark eyes were already scanning the surroundings, rifle at the ready.

"Chang, you're with me. We'll secure the upper floor," Arthur continued, glancing at their tech expert. Chang's fingers were flying over a tablet, likely already hacking local security systems.

As Jenkins secured the grappling hook, Arthur's mind raced through contingencies. 'If we can't hold this position, we'll need an alternate escape route,' he thought, studying the building's layout.

"Move out," Arthur ordered, leading the ascent. The rusted metal groaned under their weight, each step a gamble. 'Just a little further,' he urged silently, acutely aware of the exposed position they were in.

Reaching the top, Arthur pulled himself over the ledge, immediately dropping into a defensive stance. His instincts screamed danger, but the floor appeared empty.

"Clear," he whispered, helping Chang up. "Now, let's turn this deathtrap into our advantage."

Arthur's eyes darted to his watch, its digital face glowing ominously in the dim light. "We've got seven minutes before the security system resets," he said, voice low and urgent. "After that, this place will light up like Times Square on New Year's."

The weight of their mission pressed down on him. Failure wasn't an option; if they didn't secure the intel hidden in this building, countless lives would be at stake.

"Chang, I need you on that mainframe. Decrypt and download everything you can," Arthur instructed, his calm tone belying the tension coiling in his gut. "Jenkins, rig the room. If we can't take it with us, no one gets it."

As his team moved with practiced precision, Arthur's mind raced through scenarios. 'If Chang can't crack it in time, we'll have to physically extract the drives. Risky, but necessary.'

"Ramirez, what's our perimeter look like?" he asked into his comm.

"Two patrols approaching from the east, sir. ETA three minutes," came the swift reply.

Arthur nodded, though Ramirez couldn't see him. "Copy that. Keep me posted on any changes."

He turned to Chang, who was furiously typing away. "Status?"

"Firewall's tougher than expected, sir," Chang replied, sweat beading on his brow. "But I'm making progress."

"You've got four minutes," Arthur said, his voice steady despite the growing pressure. "Jenkins, how's that demolition coming?"

"Almost set, boss. This place'll be confetti if we need it to be."

Arthur allowed himself a grim smile. 'Good. At least we have that ace up our sleeve.'

He moved to the window, scanning the streets below. 'Come on, team,' he thought. 'We've faced worse. We can do this.'

Arthur's eyes narrowed as he spotted movement in the shadows below. "Incoming," he hissed, signaling his team to take cover. The sound of heavy boots echoed through the corridor outside.

"Chang, time's up. Grab what you can," Arthur ordered, his mind already formulating a new plan. "Jenkins, those charges ready?"

"Armed and waiting, sir," Jenkins whispered back.

Arthur assessed their surroundings, his gaze landing on the ventilation shaft above. "New exit strategy. We're going up and over."

As the footsteps grew louder, Arthur grabbed a nearby chair, dragging it silently beneath the vent. With practiced efficiency, he unscrewed the grate, his fingers working swiftly.

THE EXTRACTION

"Sir, the data—" Chang started, worry evident in his voice.

"No time," Arthur cut him off. "We adapt. Jenkins, your demo kit. Now."

Understanding dawned on Jenkins' face as he handed over the compact bag. Arthur quickly rigged a makeshift pulley system using the kit's rope and carabiners.

"Chang, you first. Take the drive. Jenkins, cover our six," Arthur commanded, his voice low but firm.

As Chang disappeared into the vent, Arthur turned to Jenkins. "Once we're clear, trigger the charges. That'll buy us some time and destroy what we couldn't take."

The door handle jiggled. Arthur's muscles tensed, ready for action. "Move, now!"

Jenkins scrambled up the rope as Arthur covered their escape. Just as the door burst open, Arthur pulled himself into the vent, yanking the grate shut behind him.

'Not ideal,' he thought, crawling through the cramped space, 'but we're still in the game.'

Arthur's shoulders scraped against the narrow vent as he crawled forward, the metal cool beneath his palms. Ahead, he could hear Chang's labored breathing and Jenkins' muttered curses.

"Status," Arthur whispered, his voice barely audible over the distant shouts echoing through the facility.

"Clear so far, boss," Jenkins replied, his tone clipped.

Arthur felt a presence behind him and turned his head slightly, catching sight of Jose Beals bringing up the rear. Their eyes met briefly, and Arthur noticed a flicker of something—resentment, perhaps—in Jose's gaze.

"Beals, any pursuit?" Arthur asked, keeping his voice neutral.

"Negative," Jose replied, his jaw clenched. "But we're leaving a trail. They'll figure it out soon enough."

THE EXTRACTION

Arthur's mind raced, weighing their options. "We need to split up. Chang, take the north route with Jenkins. Beals and I will create a diversion."

As they reached a junction in the ventilation system, Arthur caught Jose's arm. "You good with this?"

Jose's eyes narrowed. "Always am, aren't I? It's what I'm here for."

The tension between them was palpable, but Arthur pushed it aside. "Let's move."

As Chang and Jenkins disappeared down one shaft, Arthur and Jose took the other. They hadn't gone far when a muffled explosion rocked the building.

"Jenkins' parting gift," Arthur muttered, a grim smile tugging at his lips.

Suddenly, the vent beneath them creaked ominously. Arthur's instincts screamed danger. "Beals, move!"

They scrambled forward just as the section behind them gave way, crashing to the floor below. Arthur's heart pounded as he peered through the gap, seeing armed guards swarming the room.

"That was too close," he thought, adrenaline surging through his veins. "We need an exit strategy, fast."

Arthur's eyes darted around, searching for an escape route. The ventilation shaft ahead was their only option, but it was rapidly filling with acrid smoke.

"Masks on," he ordered, voice low and urgent. "We push through."

Jose nodded, pulling his respirator into place. They crawled forward, the metal beneath their hands growing hotter with each passing second.

Muffled shouts and gunfire echoed from below. Arthur's mind raced, calculating their position relative to the building's layout.

"Two more junctions," he thought. "Then we're out."

Suddenly, a burst of gunfire pierced the vent directly beneath them. Arthur instinctively flattened himself, feeling the heat of bullets passing inches from his face.

"Move!" he hissed to Jose, pushing forward with renewed urgency.

They scrambled through the smoke-filled shaft, lungs burning despite the masks. Arthur's muscles screamed in protest, but he forced himself onward.

As they approached the final turn, a deafening explosion rocked the building. The vent buckled, twisting metal shrieking around them.

"Jump!" Arthur shouted, kicking out the nearest vent cover.

Without hesitation, he launched himself into open air, Jose right behind him. They hit the ground rolling, debris raining down around them.

Arthur sprang to his feet, assessing their surroundings. They were on a narrow ledge, a sheer drop on one side and flames licking at the building's exterior on the other.

"Options?" Jose asked, voice tense.

Arthur's gaze locked onto a maintenance crane nearby, its arm extending just within reach.

"We jump," he said, already moving. "Now or never, Beals."

As they sprinted towards the edge, the ledge began to crumble beneath their feet. Arthur leapt, arm outstretched, fingers grasping for the crane's metal frame.

Arthur's hand clamped onto the crane's cold steel, muscles straining as he swung his body. He glanced back to see Jose barely make the jump, grabbing onto Arthur's boot.

"Hold tight," Arthur grunted, assessing their precarious position.

The crane groaned under their combined weight. Arthur's mind raced, plotting their next move. They couldn't stay here long.

"There," he said, nodding towards a rusty access ladder on the building's side. "We need to reach that ladder. It's our only way down."

Jose's voice was strained. "How? It's at least ten feet away."

THE EXTRACTION

Arthur's eyes narrowed, scanning their surroundings. A coil of rope hung from the crane's arm, just within reach.

"I've got an idea," he said. "But you're not going to like it."

Without waiting for a response, Arthur reached out, snagging the rope. He quickly fashioned a makeshift harness, looping it around Jose's waist.

"When I give the signal, you're going to swing," Arthur instructed. "Use the momentum to reach the ladder."

Jose's eyes widened. "Are you insane? What about you?"

Arthur's jaw clenched. "I'll be right behind you. Trust me."

He could see the doubt in Jose's eyes, but there was no time for debate. Arthur began to swing the crane arm, building momentum.

"Now!" he shouted.

Jose let go, arcing through the air. For a heart-stopping moment, it seemed he wouldn't make it. Then his hands grasped the ladder rungs.

Arthur allowed himself a brief sigh of relief before focusing on his own escape. The crane was becoming increasingly unstable.

"Your turn, old man," he muttered to himself, preparing for the leap.

As he tensed to jump, a sudden explosion rocked the building. The crane lurched violently, nearly dislodging Arthur's grip.

"Arthur!" Jose yelled from the ladder. "Jump!"

Gritting his teeth, Arthur launched himself towards the ladder, time seeming to slow as he sailed through the air.

Arthur's fingers grazed the cold metal of the ladder, nearly slipping off before he managed to secure his grip. The impact sent shockwaves through his arms, but he held on, adrenaline surging through his veins.

"Nice catch," Jose grunted, already climbing down.

"Save the compliments," Arthur replied, his voice taut. "We're not out of this yet."

As they descended, Arthur's mind raced, assessing their next move. The explosion meant their window of opportunity was rapidly closing.

"Eli, status report," he barked into his comm.

Eli's voice crackled through, tense but controlled. "Hostiles converging on your position. ETA two minutes. Extraction point is compromised."

Arthur's jaw clenched. "Virginia, we need an alternate route."

"Working on it," came her clipped response. "There's a maintenance tunnel 200 meters east. It'll be tight, but it should lead you to the outskirts."

They reached the ground, Arthur's knees protesting as he landed. He scanned the area, spotting the tunnel entrance partially hidden behind a stack of rusty containers.

"Move," he ordered Jose, breaking into a sprint.

As they ran, the sound of shouting and gunfire erupted behind them. Arthur's mind flashed to Ali, wondering if their enigmatic ally had made it out or if he'd been the source of the explosion.

They reached the tunnel, Jose diving in first. Arthur paused at the entrance, drawing his sidearm.

"Go," he told Jose. "I'll cover our six."

Jose hesitated. "Arthur-"

"That's an order, soldier," Arthur growled, his piercing eyes brooking no argument.

As Jose disappeared into the darkness, Arthur took a deep breath, steeling himself for what was to come. The mission wasn't over – far from it. But as he heard the approaching footsteps of their pursuers, a grim smile tugged at his lips.

"Let's see what you've got," he muttered, raising his weapon and preparing to face whatever came next.

CHAPTER 2

The fluorescent lights buzzed overhead as Arthur Duggins surveyed his team, their faces etched with grim determination. The secure briefing room felt like a pressure cooker, tension building with each passing second. Duggins' eyes darted to the reinforced door, his jaw clenching imperceptibly.

"Stay sharp," he murmured, his voice low and steady. The team responded with barely perceptible nods, their postures rigid and alert.

Duggins' mind raced, analyzing potential scenarios. What new hell would Virginia Turner unleash upon them this time? He'd learned long ago that her calm exterior often masked a storm of calculated ambition.

The door swung open with a soft hiss, and Virginia Turner strode in, her presence immediately commanding the room. Duggins' gaze locked onto her piercing blue eyes, searching for any hint of her true intentions.

"Gentlemen," Virginia greeted, her voice smooth as silk. She moved with practiced grace, each step measured and purposeful.

Duggins couldn't help but notice the impeccable cut of her tailored suit, a subtle reminder of the power she wielded. He tensed, preparing for the verbal sparring match that was sure to come.

"Ms. Turner," he acknowledged, his tone clipped. "I trust you have a good reason for calling us in on such short notice."

Virginia's lips curled into a smile that didn't quite reach her eyes. "Oh, Arthur. When have I ever wasted your time?"

Duggins felt a flicker of irritation. He knew her game all too well – the dance of half-truths and calculated revelations. He leaned forward, hands clasped on the table.

"Cut the pleasantries, Virginia. What's the situation?"

She arched an eyebrow, clearly savoring the moment. "Impatient as always, I see. Very well, let's get down to business."

As Virginia began to speak, Duggins studied her carefully, searching for any tell that might betray her true motives. He knew the stakes were high – they always were – but something about this felt different. More dangerous.

Whatever Virginia had in store for them, Duggins silently vowed to keep his team safe. No matter the cost.

Virginia's piercing blue eyes swept the room, commanding attention. "Gentlemen, we have an imminent threat to Tel Aviv. A terrorist attack of unprecedented scale is in its final stages."

Duggins felt his pulse quicken. The urgency in Virginia's voice was unmistakable.

She continued, her tone sharp and focused, "Our intel suggests we have less than 72 hours to prevent a catastrophe that could destabilize the entire region."

"What's the source?" Duggins interjected, his mind already racing through potential scenarios.

Virginia's lips tightened almost imperceptibly. "That brings me to our key player. Ali Shabaab."

The name hung in the air, heavy with implications. Duggins leaned forward, his interest piqued.

"Shabaab is a ghost," Virginia explained, her voice lowering. "A man with deep ties to every major terrorist cell in the Middle East. He's agreed to provide us with critical intelligence, but extracting him won't be easy."

Duggins' eyes narrowed. "And we're sure he's legit? This isn't some elaborate trap?"

Virginia's gaze locked onto his, unflinching. "Shabaab's information has already prevented two attacks. He's our best chance at stopping this one."

Duggins couldn't shake the feeling that there was more to this story. He watched Virginia carefully, searching for any cracks in her composure. But her mask remained firmly in place, revealing nothing but steely determination.

As Virginia delved deeper into the briefing, Duggins found himself caught between the urgency of the mission and the nagging doubt about Shabaab's true motives. One thing was certain – this was going to be one hell of a dangerous game.

Duggins glanced around the room, gauging his team's reactions. Their faces had hardened into masks of grim determination, jaws clenched and eyes focused. He recognized that look – it was the same one he'd seen countless times before high-stakes operations. A mixture of adrenaline, fear, and unwavering resolve.

Captain Sarah Reeves, his second-in-command, caught his eye and gave a slight nod. Her usually jovial demeanor had vanished, replaced by the steel-eyed focus of a seasoned operator. Beside her, Tech Specialist Mike Chen's fingers twitched, likely already running through the necessary equipment checks in his mind.

Duggins felt a swell of pride. This was why he trusted these people with his life. Their loyalty to the mission, to each other, was unshakeable.

He turned back to Virginia, his voice low but firm. "Ms. Turner, while I appreciate the urgency, we need to discuss contingencies. What if Shabaab isn't what he claims to be?"

Virginia's eyes flashed. "Are you questioning our intelligence, Mr. Duggins?"

"I'm questioning everything," he replied evenly. "That's my job. We've seen double agents before, and the stakes here are too high to take anything at face value."

"Your caution is noted," Virginia said, her tone clipped. "But we don't have time for paranoia. Every minute we waste could cost lives in Tel Aviv."

Duggins leaned in, his voice dropping to a near-whisper. "And every minute we rush could lead us into a trap that costs even more. I need to know you've considered all angles here."

The tension between them crackled, two immovable forces locked in a silent battle of wills.

Virginia's piercing blue eyes narrowed as she met Duggins' gaze. "Your concerns are misplaced, Mr. Duggins," she said, her voice laced with a calm certainty that only deepened Arthur's unease. "Our intelligence is rock solid. Ali-Shabaab's information has been independently verified through multiple channels. The team's abilities, combined with this intel, make success all but guaranteed."

Duggins felt his jaw tighten. The dismissal was too quick, too absolute. It reeked of overconfidence – or something worse. He opened his mouth to argue further, but Virginia had already turned away, addressing the room at large.

"Prepare for immediate deployment," she ordered. "Time is of the essence."

THE EXTRACTION

As the team sprang into action, Duggins pushed his misgivings aside, focusing on the task at hand. He strode to the equipment locker, methodically checking each piece of gear.

"Run it down for me, Chen," he said, slipping on his tactical vest.

Mike's fingers flew over his tablet. "Comms are encrypted and synced. Satellite uplink is green. I've loaded the latest structural plans of our target building onto everyone's devices."

Duggins nodded, his mind racing. Something about this didn't add up, but right now, his team needed his full attention. He watched as Sarah expertly field-stripped and reassembled her rifle, her movements fluid and practiced.

"How're we looking on ordnance?" he asked.

Sarah's reply was crisp. "Full loadout, boss. Non-lethal options included, as requested."

As he holstered his sidearm, Duggins couldn't shake the nagging doubt Virginia's dismissal had planted. 'What am I missing?' he thought, scanning the room. His team was ready, their professionalism evident in every precise movement. But were they walking into something they couldn't prepare for?

Duggins took a deep breath, steeling himself. His team needed him now, more than ever. He cleared his throat, drawing their attention.

"Listen up," he said, his voice low but commanding. The room fell silent, all eyes on him. "What we're about to do... it's not just another mission. We're racing against the clock to prevent a catastrophe that could claim thousands of innocent lives."

He paused, meeting each team member's gaze. "I know you've all got questions. Hell, I've got plenty myself. But right now, we need to focus on the task at hand. Ali-Shabaab is our key to unraveling this mess, and we're the only ones who can get to him."

Duggins' mind raced, analyzing every angle of their approach. "Mike, I want real-time satellite feeds the moment we touch down. Sarah, you're on overwatch – any sign of trouble, you sing out immediately. Chen, keep our comms airtight. If anyone so much as sneezes in Baghdad, I want to know about it."

He could see the determination hardening in their eyes, feeding off his own resolve. "We're walking into the unknown here, people. Trust your instincts, watch each other's backs, and remember – hesitation gets you killed. Clear?"

A chorus of affirmatives rang out. Duggins nodded, a grim smile tugging at his lips. "Good. Gear up and move out. We've got a world to save."

As the team made their final preparations, Duggins found himself studying the briefing room one last time. The air was thick with anticipation, tinged with the faint smell of gun oil and nervous sweat. He watched his team, noting the set of their jaws, the focused glint in their eyes.

'We're ready,' he thought, 'but for what?' The question nagged at him as he shouldered his pack. Whatever lay ahead in Baghdad, Duggins knew one thing for certain – they'd face it together, come hell or high water.

The team moved with practiced efficiency, their footsteps echoing through the corridor as they made their way to the waiting transport vehicles. Duggins felt the familiar surge of adrenaline coursing through his veins, his senses sharpening with each step.

"Jose," he called out, falling in step with his second-in-command. "I need your eyes on Ali Shabaab the moment we land. Something about this doesn't sit right."

Jose nodded, his face a mask of concentration. "You think he might flip on us?"

"I think we can't afford to take any chances," Duggins replied, his voice low. "This whole op feels off-balance. Virginia's pushing too hard, too fast."

As they approached the vehicles, the team's anticipation was palpable. Mike was double-checking his tech gear, muttering calculations under his breath. Sarah's fingers drummed a nervous rhythm on her rifle stock, her eyes scanning the perimeter out of habit.

Duggins paused at the transport's open door, taking one last look at his team. The weight of responsibility settled heavily on his shoulders. 'How many of us will make it back?' he wondered, pushing the thought aside as quickly as it came.

"Alright, people," he announced, his voice cutting through the tension. "Once we're wheels up, there's no turning back. Baghdad's waiting, and so are our friends in Ali-Shabaab's network. Stay sharp, stay alive."

With a final nod to his team, Duggins climbed into the transport. As the doors sealed shut and the engines roared to life, he allowed himself a moment of quiet reflection. Whatever dangers awaited them in Baghdad, whatever secrets Ali Shabaab held, Duggins knew that the next few hours would test them all to their limits.

The transport lurched forward, carrying them towards an uncertain future and the promise of imminent peril. Duggins closed his eyes, took a deep breath, and steeled himself for the challenges ahead. The game was on, and the stakes had never been higher.

CHAPTER 3

The dim glow of tactical flashlights illuminated the cramped safehouse basement, casting long shadows across the faces of the C.O.R.E. team. Arthur Duggins methodically disassembled his M4 carbine, his calloused fingers moving with practiced precision. The familiar scent of gun oil filled his nostrils as he inspected each component, his piercing eyes scrutinizing every detail.

"Comms check," Duggins ordered, his voice low and gravelly.

A chorus of affirmatives crackled through his earpiece. Satisfied, he reassembled his weapon with swift, economical movements. The weight of responsibility settled on his shoulders as he surveyed his team, each member absorbed in their own meticulous preparations.

Duggins cleared his throat, drawing their attention. "Listen up," he commanded, his tone steady and authoritative. "Our intel suggests the target is being held in a heavily fortified compound on the outskirts of Narvik. We have a narrow window to extract the package and exfil before reinforcements arrive."

He activated a holographic display, revealing a 3D map of the area. "Our insertion point is here," he said, indicating a patch of dense forest. "We'll approach on foot to avoid detection. Once inside, we split into two teams."

THE EXTRACTION

Duggins paused, his gaze sweeping across the room. He could see the tension in their eyes, the subtle shifts in posture that betrayed their anxiety. He'd led these men and women through hell before, but this mission felt different. The stakes were higher, the margin for error razor-thin.

Don't let them see your own doubts, he reminded himself. *They need your strength now more than ever.*

"I won't sugarcoat it," Duggins continued, his voice resolute. "This op is high-risk. We're dealing with an unknown number of hostiles, potential traps, and a ticking clock. But I've seen what this team can do. We're the best of the best, and failure is not an option."

As he spoke, Duggins felt a familiar surge of adrenaline coursing through his veins. The pre-mission jitters transformed into a laser-like focus, his mind already racing through contingencies and worst-case scenarios.

"Any questions?" he asked, scanning the room one last time.

The silence that followed spoke volumes. His team was ready, their faces set with grim determination. Duggins nodded, a surge of pride momentarily displacing his concerns.

"Gear up," he ordered. "We move out in five."

Jose Beals stepped forward, his muscular frame tense. "Sir, what about our exit strategy? If things go sideways, we'll be deep in hostile territory with limited support."

Duggins nodded, appreciating Jose's tactical mindset. "Good question. We'll have a chopper on standby at these coordinates," he said, pointing to a map. "If comms go dark, make your way there. It's our fallback point."

Ali Shabaab, who had been silent until now, spoke up. His measured tone carried an undercurrent of tension. "And what of the potential double agent? Do we have a plan to identify and neutralize the threat?"

The room fell silent, all eyes turning to Duggins. He met Ali's piercing gaze, weighing his response carefully. "We operate on a need-to-know basis. Trust no one outside this room. If you suspect someone's compromised, use the coded phrase we discussed."

Jose's jaw clenched. "With all due respect, sir, that's not much of a plan. We're walking into a hornets' nest blind."

THE EXTRACTION

Duggins felt the weight of their concerns, his own unease mirrored in their faces. He took a deep breath, choosing his next words carefully. "I understand your reservations. But remember, we've trained for this. Our success depends on our ability to adapt and overcome. Stay alert, trust your instincts, and watch each other's backs."

As the team continued to discuss strategies, Duggins found himself studying Ali. The man's calm demeanor seemed at odds with the gravity of the situation. *What are you hiding?* Duggins wondered, pushing the thought aside. Now wasn't the time for suspicion. They needed to be united.

"One last thing," Duggins added, his voice cutting through the murmur of conversation. "Those surveillance systems we detected? They're top-of-the-line. We'll need to move fast and silent. Any slip-up could trigger the entire compound."

The team nodded, their expressions a mix of determination and apprehension. As they resumed their preparations, Duggins felt the familiar weight of command settling on his shoulders. *No matter what happens,* he vowed silently, *I'm bringing every one of them home.*

Duggins surveyed his team, his keen eyes assessing each member's readiness. The risks of the mission weighed heavily on his mind, but he couldn't let that show. "Listen up," he said, his voice low and steady. "We're facing unknown variables here. Enemy strength, potential moles, advanced security systems. But remember, we're the best at what we do."

As he spoke, Duggins watched his team's reactions closely. *They're tense, but focused. Good.* He continued, "Our adaptability is our greatest asset. Stay alert, communicate, and trust your training."

While Duggins addressed the team, Sarah began prepping her stealth suit, the matte black material designed to absorb light and heat signatures. "Boss," she interjected, "what's our contingency if the intel on guard rotations is off?"

Duggins nodded, appreciating her foresight. "We stick to shadows, use natural cover. If cornered, non-lethal takedowns only. We can't risk raising alarms."

As he spoke, Duggins moved to check his own gear. He adjusted the straps on his tactical vest, ensuring a snug fit. *One loose strap could mean the difference between life and death,* he reminded himself.

"Jose, how are those comms looking?" Duggins asked, turning to the team's tech specialist.

THE EXTRACTION

Jose held up a sleek, almost invisible earpiece. "State of the art, boss. Encrypted channels, long-range capability. We'll maintain contact even if we're forced to split up."

Duggins nodded approvingly, his mind already racing through potential scenarios. *If communications fail, we're in trouble. But we've trained for this. We're ready.*

"Good work," he said aloud. "Everyone, final equipment check. Night vision, stealth gear, non-lethal options. We move in ten."

The muffled clicks of safeties being disengaged and magazines sliding into place filled the dimly lit room. Duggins ran his hands over his M4 carbine, fingers dancing across the weapon with practiced precision. He checked the sight alignment, tested the trigger pull, and ensured the suppressor was securely attached.

"Weapons hot, people," Duggins commanded, his voice low and steady. "Double-check your loads and backups."

Jose hefted his compact submachine gun, eyes narrowed in concentration. "Full mag, one in the chamber," he reported, then patted his vest. "Two spare mags, plus sidearm."

Eli, ever the silent professional, merely nodded as he finished inspecting his sniper rifle. His blue eyes, usually hidden behind sunglasses, now gleamed with laser-like focus.

"Alright team, positions and formations," Duggins said, spreading a tactical map on a nearby crate. "Eli, you're our eyes. I want you here," he pointed to a elevated position overlooking the compound. "Jose, you're on point. Sarah and I will flank."

Jose leaned in, studying the map intently. "What's our approach vector, boss?"

Duggins traced a path with his finger. "We'll use the ravine for cover, then split at this junction. Questions?"

Eli spoke up, his voice barely above a whisper. "Contingency for potential sentries at the north entrance?"

"Good catch," Duggins nodded, appreciating Eli's attention to detail. "If we encounter resistance there, we'll divert to the east. It's less direct, but offers better concealment."

As the team huddled around the map, Duggins felt a familiar tension coiling in his gut. *So many variables, so much that could go wrong,* he thought. *But we've planned for every contingency. We're ready.*

THE EXTRACTION

"Remember," Duggins said, meeting each team member's gaze, "flexibility is key. Stick to the plan, but be prepared to adapt. Clear?"

A chorus of affirmatives answered him, each voice carrying the weight of their shared responsibility.

Duggins straightened, his eyes scanning each member of his team. "Listen up," he began, his voice low but commanding. "Communication is our lifeline out there. One slip, one moment of radio silence, and we're compromised."

Sarah's hand tightened on her rifle. "What if we lose contact?" she asked, her tone betraying a hint of concern.

"Then we fall back on our training," Duggins replied, his gaze steady. "We trust each other. Every decision, every move we make affects the whole team. We're only as strong as our weakest link."

Jose nodded, his usually jovial face now set in grim determination. "We've got each other's backs. Always have, always will."

Duggins felt a swell of pride. *This is why we're the best,* he thought. *Not just skill, but trust.*

"Remember," he continued, "in the field, we're more than a team. We're family. Your life depends on the person next to you, and theirs on you. Understood?"

A chorus of affirmatives echoed through the room.

As the weight of the impending mission settled over them, Duggins watched his team fall into a moment of silent reflection. Sarah closed her eyes, her lips moving in a silent prayer. Eli's fingers tapped a rhythmic pattern on his rifle, a calming technique Duggins had observed before. Jose stood stock-still, his breathing slow and measured.

Duggins felt his own pulse quicken. *So much at stake,* he thought. *But we're ready. We have to be.*

He allowed himself a brief moment to consider the gravity of their task, the lives that hung in the balance. Then, with a deep breath, he pushed those thoughts aside, focusing on the mission ahead.

"Alright," Duggins said, breaking the silence. "It's time. Let's move out."

THE EXTRACTION

Duggins' voice cut through the air like a knife. "Gear up and form up. We move in two."

The team snapped into action, a well-oiled machine set in motion. Ali Shabaab moved with fluid grace, his hands deftly securing straps and checking equipment. His eyes, ever-watchful, darted between his teammates as he fell into formation.

Jose Beals hefted his assault rifle, muscles rippling beneath his tactical gear. He rolled his shoulders, a fleeting grimace crossing his face. *Old wounds never truly heal*, Duggins thought, noting the gesture.

Virginia Turner was the last to join the line, her manicured hands looking oddly out of place as she adjusted her body armor. Her blue eyes met Duggins', a silent challenge in their depths.

"Remember," Duggins said, his voice low and intense, "once we're in that transport, we're in enemy territory. Stay sharp, stay quiet."

The team moved as one towards the waiting vehicle, its dark bulk a promise of the dangers to come. Duggins felt the familiar tightening in his gut, the mix of anticipation and dread that preceded every mission.

As they approached the transport, Jose muttered, "Anyone else feel like we're walking into the lion's den?"

"More like the snake pit," Ali replied, his voice barely above a whisper.

Virginia's lips curved into a thin smile. "Snakes, lions... we've faced worse."

Duggins raised an eyebrow at the exchange. *Tension's high*, he noted. *Got to keep them focused.*

"Cut the chatter," he ordered as they reached the vehicle. "Board up, now."

One by one, they climbed into the transport's dark interior. Duggins watched their faces as they settled in – determination etched in every line, fear hidden behind masks of resolve.

As he took his own seat, Duggins caught a glimpse of his reflection in the window. The face that stared back at him was weathered, lined with the weight of countless missions. *How many more?* he wondered. *How long before our luck runs out?*

But there was no time for such thoughts. The transport's engine roared to life, and with it, the reality of their mission crashed over them like a wave. They were committed now, for better or worse.

Duggins took a deep breath, pushing aside his doubts. "Lock and load," he commanded, his voice steady despite the turmoil in his gut. "It's showtime."

As the transport rumbled to life, Duggins caught Eli's eye. The veteran operative gave him a subtle nod, his piercing blue gaze conveying a silent message of support. Duggins returned the gesture, feeling a surge of confidence.

"Remember," Duggins said, his voice low but firm, "we're only as strong as our weakest link. Watch each other's backs out there."

Jose leaned forward, his muscular frame taut with anticipation. "Like a well-oiled machine, boss. We've got this."

Raven, seated in the corner, spoke up with measured precision. "Contingencies in place for all scenarios. We're prepared for whatever comes our way."

The transport lurched forward, its tires crunching on gravel as it pulled away from the secure compound. Duggins felt the familiar tightening in his chest, a mix of adrenaline and apprehension that always preceded a high-stakes mission.

This is it, he thought, his mind racing through potential outcomes. *No turning back now.*

As the vehicle picked up speed, heading towards the unknown dangers that awaited them, Duggins allowed himself a moment of introspection. *We're ready. We have to be.*

The team fell into a tense silence, each member lost in their own thoughts as the transport carried them inexorably towards their objective. The weight of their mission hung heavy in the air, a palpable presence that bound them together in shared purpose and resolve.

Suddenly, the transport lurched violently, throwing the team off balance. A deafening explosion rocked the air, and the acrid smell of burning rubber filled the cabin.

"We're hit!" Jose shouted, his hand already on his weapon.

Duggins' mind raced. "Everyone, positions! Ali, status report!"

THE EXTRACTION

Ali's fingers flew across a handheld device. "Roadside IED. Driver's unconscious. We're sitting ducks out here."

Virginia's voice cut through the chaos, cool and collected. "Hostiles approaching from the north. ETA two minutes."

Duggins felt time slow as he processed the situation. They were exposed, their carefully laid plans already unraveling. He caught Raven's eye, searching for any sign that this was part of some larger scheme, but the Phantom Broker's face remained impassive.

"We abort, regroup at checkpoint Charlie," Duggins ordered, his voice steady despite the turmoil in his gut.

Jose tensed beside him. "Arthur, if we pull back now-"

"We're compromised," Duggins cut him off, making the call he knew could haunt him. "Everyone out, defensive formation. Move!"

As the team scrambled to exit the disabled transport, Duggins couldn't shake the feeling that they were walking into something far more dangerous than they'd anticipated. The mission, their very lives, now balanced on a knife's edge.

How the hell did they know we were coming? The thought burned in his mind as he readied his weapon, the sound of approaching vehicles growing louder with each passing second.

CHAPTER 4

The fluorescent light flickered overhead, casting harsh shadows across the weathered faces of the two men seated at the metal table. Arthur Duggins leaned forward, his scarred hands clasped tightly before him. His piercing gaze bore into Eli Cohen, searching for any hint of deception.

"What's the latest on Ali-Shabaab?" Duggins asked, his voice low and gravelly. "Any movement we should be aware of?"

Cohen's lips twitched, the ghost of a smile playing at the corners of his mouth. He removed his sunglasses, revealing eyes as sharp and cold as steel. "Always straight to business, eh, Arthur?"

Duggins didn't flinch. "Time isn't a luxury we have, Eli. You know that as well as I do."

The safehouse creaked and groaned around them, a discordant symphony of settling wood and rusted pipes. Duggins' mind raced, analyzing every micro-expression that crossed Cohen's face. *Can I trust him? Even after all these years?*

Cohen leaned back, his chair scraping against the concrete floor. "Our target's been busy. Moving between locations, never staying in one place for long."

"Specifics, Cohen. I need specifics." Duggins' fingers drummed an impatient rhythm on the table's surface.

"Patience, my friend," Cohen chided, his voice silky smooth. "You know I always deliver."

Duggins fought to keep his frustration in check. Cohen's games were infuriating, but his intel was usually spot-on. Still, the stakes were too high for half-truths and misdirection.

"Lives are on the line," Duggins growled. "Every second we waste here is another second Ali-Shabaab has to slip through our fingers."

Cohen's eyes narrowed, a flicker of something—respect, perhaps?—passing through them. "You're right, of course. But rushing in blind is a surefire way to get us all killed."

Duggins nodded, grudgingly acknowledging the point. He took a deep breath, forcing his tense muscles to relax. "Alright, Eli. Tell me what you know. Every detail, no matter how small."

As Cohen began to speak, Duggins listened intently, his analytical mind already piecing together the fragments of information.

Whatever came next, he knew one thing for certain: the hunt for Ali-Shabaab was about to reach its endgame.

Cohen leaned forward, his voice dropping to a low, intense murmur. "Ali-Shabaab's been spotted in the outskirts of Baghdad. Remote area, mostly abandoned buildings. He's jumping between safehouses like a man possessed."

Duggins' eyes narrowed, his mind racing. "How often is he moving?"

"Every 12 to 24 hours," Cohen replied, a hint of admiration in his tone. "He's paranoid, but smart. Makes him a damn difficult target."

Duggins nodded, processing the information. His fingers tapped a staccato rhythm on the table as he considered the implications. "Any pattern to his movements?"

Cohen shook his head. "Nothing predictable. But we've identified three locations he seems to favor."

As Cohen pulled out a map, Duggins leaned in, studying the marked locations. His mind was already formulating potential strategies, weighing risks against rewards.

"What about the local landscape?" Duggins asked, his gaze still fixed on the map. "Any rival factions we need to worry about?"

Cohen's lips twitched in a ghost of a smile. "Now you're asking the right questions, Arthur."

Duggins looked up, meeting Cohen's piercing blue eyes. "I always do, Eli. It's why I'm still alive."

Cohen's smile faded, his expression growing grave. He leaned in closer, voice dropping to a near-whisper. "There's something else you need to know, Arthur. We've uncovered evidence of double agents within military intelligence."

Duggins felt his muscles tense, a chill running down his spine. He maintained his outward composure, but his mind raced, reassessing every piece of information he'd received. "How deep does it go?" he asked, voice low and controlled.

Cohen's eyes darted around the room before settling back on Duggins. "We're not sure. But it's enough to compromise our mission if we're not careful."

Duggins leaned back, running a hand through his hair. The weight of this new information settled heavily on his shoulders. He'd faced dangers before, but traitors within their own ranks added a whole new level of complexity.

"This changes everything," Duggins muttered, more to himself than to Cohen. He looked up, eyes hardening with resolve. "Infiltrating enemy territory is risky enough. With double agents in play, we're walking into a potential minefield."

Cohen nodded solemnly. "Every step we take, every piece of intel we receive, we'll have to question. It's a dangerous game, Arthur."

Duggins' mind whirled with potential scenarios, each more perilous than the last. "We'll need to create a separate, secure channel of communication," he said, his tactical mind already seeking solutions. "And we can't trust anyone outside this room. Not until we know who's compromised."

As the gravity of the situation settled over them, Duggins couldn't shake the feeling that they were about to step into the lion's den – blindfolded.

Cohen leaned forward, his piercing blue eyes locked onto Duggins. "Arthur, I understand your concerns. They're valid. But let me assure you, we can navigate these treacherous waters." His voice carried a quiet confidence that seemed to fill the room.

Duggins' brow furrowed, skepticism etched across his face. "How can you be so certain?"

Cohen's lips curled into a knowing smile. "Because I've done this dance before. My sources... they're not just reliable, they're indispensable. Cultivated over years, tested in fire."

Duggins watched as Cohen's hand moved to his chest pocket, withdrawing a small, innocuous-looking device. "This," Cohen explained, "is our ace. It's a quantum encryption module. Unbreakable, even to our own agencies."

Duggins leaned in, intrigued despite his reservations. His mind raced, considering the implications. If Cohen was right, this could change everything.

"I've faced double agents before, Arthur," Cohen continued, his voice dropping to barely above a whisper. "Tehran, '09. Mogadishu, '14. Each time, we adapted, we survived, we succeeded."

Duggins felt a grudging respect growing. Cohen's experience was undeniable, his resources impressive. Still, a nagging doubt persisted.

"And Ali-Shabaab?" Duggins probed. "You're certain we can extract him, even with these complications?"

Cohen's eyes glinted with determination. "More than certain. With your tactical expertise and my intelligence network, we're the best shot he's got."

Duggins exhaled slowly, weighing the risks against the potential payoff. His instincts, honed over years in the field, told him this was their best option. Perhaps their only option.

"Alright, Cohen," Duggins said finally, extending his hand across the table. "Let's do this. Together."

As their hands clasped, Duggins couldn't shake the feeling that he was making a deal with the devil. But sometimes, to navigate hell, you needed a guide who knew the terrain.

Duggins leaned forward, his calloused fingers tracing the outline of the compound on the satellite imagery spread before them. "Three entry points," he murmured, his voice low and focused. "Heavy fortifications on the north and east sides. Our best bet is coming in from the southwest."

Cohen nodded, his piercing blue eyes scanning the map. "My intel suggests a shift change at 0200 hours. That's our window."

Duggins felt the familiar surge of adrenaline, his mind already piecing together a plan. "We'll need a diversion," he mused, more to himself than Cohen. "Something to draw their attention away from the southwest corner."

"I might have just the thing," Cohen replied, a hint of a smile playing at the corners of his mouth. He pulled out a small, cylindrical device from his jacket. "Sonic disruptor. Military grade. It'll create enough chaos to mask our approach."

Duggins raised an eyebrow, impressed despite himself. "That's not standard issue. Where did you get that?"

Cohen's smile widened fractionally. "Let's just say I have friends in interesting places."

Duggins nodded, filing away this piece of information for later consideration. He turned his attention back to the map, his mind racing through scenarios. "We'll need a three-man team. You and I, plus one more for extraction support. I'm thinking Martinez - she's the best pilot we've got."

"Agreed," Cohen said, his tone approving. "I can have a stealth chopper waiting five klicks south of the compound. We go in fast, grab Ali-Shabaab, and we're out before they know what hit them."

THE EXTRACTION

Duggins felt a surge of quiet confidence. This could work. It was risky, but with their combined skills and resources, they stood a fighting chance. He met Cohen's gaze, seeing his own determination mirrored there.

"It's a solid plan," Duggins said, his voice steady. "But we'll need to be prepared for anything. If Ali-Shabaab isn't where we expect him to be, or if we encounter heavier resistance than anticipated, we'll need to adapt quickly."

Cohen nodded grimly. "That's where your tactical expertise comes in, Arthur. I'll get us in, but once we're inside, it's your show."

Duggins felt the weight of responsibility settle on his shoulders, familiar and heavy. But for the first time since this mission began, he felt a glimmer of hope. They had a plan, they had the skills, and they had each other's backs. It might just be enough.

Cohen leaned forward, his piercing blue eyes locked on Duggins. "We should consider a two-pronged approach," he suggested, his voice low and precise. "While we infiltrate from the ground, Martinez could provide aerial surveillance. It'll give us real-time intel on guard movements and potential escape routes."

Duggins nodded, his mind already racing through the implications. "Smart," he muttered, fingers drumming on the table. "We could equip her with thermal imaging tech. If Ali-Shabaab tries to slip away in the chaos, we'll have eyes on him from above."

"Exactly," Cohen said, a hint of approval in his tone. "And I've got a contact who can provide us with jamming equipment. We'll cut off their communications, leaving them blind and disorganized."

Duggins felt a grudging respect for Cohen's strategic mind. The man's network of contacts and wealth of experience were proving invaluable. "Good thinking," he admitted. "We'll need to synchronize our timing down to the second. One misstep and the whole operation falls apart."

Cohen's lips quirked in a half-smile. "That's where your meticulous planning comes in, Arthur. I've seen your work - you leave nothing to chance."

As the final pieces of the plan fell into place, Duggins felt a familiar tension coiling in his gut. It was always like this before a high-stakes mission - equal parts anticipation and dread. He stood, extending his hand to Cohen.

Their eyes met as they shook hands, a silent understanding passing between them. No words were needed; they both knew the risks, the importance of what lay ahead. With a brief nod, they parted, each man's mind already racing through the preparations to come.

THE EXTRACTION

Duggins rose from his seat, muscles taut with anticipation. His mind whirred, cataloging the myriad details they'd need to address before the operation. As he turned to leave, he noticed Cohen still seated, an inscrutable expression on his face.

"Something else on your mind, Eli?" Duggins asked, his voice low and measured.

Cohen's piercing blue eyes met Duggins', a flicker of... something... passing through them. "Just considering all the angles, Arthur. It's a habit that's kept me alive this long."

Duggins felt a prickle of unease. "Care to share those angles?"

A ghost of a smile touched Cohen's lips. "Nothing concrete. Let's just say I always like to have a contingency for my contingencies."

The cryptic response set off alarm bells in Duggins' mind. He'd worked with enough spooks to know when someone was holding back. "I thought we agreed on full transparency, Cohen."

"We did," Cohen replied smoothly, rising to his feet. "And you have all the information pertinent to the mission. The rest... well, let's just say it's insurance."

Duggins' jaw tightened. "Insurance against what, exactly?"

Cohen's expression remained unreadable. "Against the unexpected, Arthur. It's a dangerous world out there."

As they moved towards the door, Duggins couldn't shake the feeling that Cohen was playing a game within a game. But now wasn't the time for doubts. They had a mission to prepare for.

"I'll have my team ready in 48 hours," Duggins said, his hand on the doorknob.

Cohen nodded. "I'll make the necessary arrangements on my end. Good hunting, Arthur."

With that, they parted ways, each man disappearing into the shadows of Baghdad's bustling streets. As Duggins melted into the crowd, his mind raced. He trusted Cohen's abilities, but the man's enigmatic nature left him with a gnawing uncertainty. Whatever happened in the coming days, Duggins knew he'd need to stay sharp – not just for the mission, but to unravel the mysteries surrounding his enigmatic partner.

CHAPTER 5

The acrid smell of smoke-filled Arthur Duggins' nostrils as he pressed his back against the cold concrete wall. His heart thundered in his chest, but his breathing remained steady, controlled. Through the comms, he heard the labored breaths of his team.

"Hostiles on your six, Martinez," Duggins whispered, his eyes darting to the heat signatures on his wrist-mounted display. "Two tangos, armed."

"Copy that," came the hushed reply.

Duggins signaled with his hand, and his team moved in perfect unison, flowing like water around obstacles. The simulation felt real – too real. Every decision could mean life or death.

"Remember, people," Duggins said, his voice low but firm. "Clean shots only. We've got civilians in the mix."

As they rounded the corner, Duggins caught sight of the hostages – training dummies with terrified expressions painted on their faces. His mind raced, analyzing angles, assessing risks.

"Beals, take point. Chen, cover our six," Duggins ordered, feeling the weight of command settle on his shoulders. He watched as his team executed the maneuver flawlessly, pride swelling in his chest.

Suddenly, a flash of movement caught his eye. "Contact!" Duggins barked, dropping to one knee and raising his weapon in one fluid motion.

The team reacted instantly, a symphony of coordinated action. Shots rang out, the sharp crack of gunfire echoing off the walls. Duggins felt the familiar surge of adrenaline, his senses heightened to a razor's edge.

As the last target fell, Duggins called out, "Status report!"

"All clear, sir," Chen responded, her voice steady despite the intensity of the moment.

Duggins nodded, allowing himself a brief moment of satisfaction. "Good work, team. But remember, in the field, we won't get second chances. Let's run it again."

As they reset the simulation, Duggins caught his reflection in a shattered window. The lines around his eyes seemed deeper, a testament to the weight of his responsibilities. He pushed the thought aside, focusing on the task at hand.

"Alright, people," he said, his voice carrying the authority of years of experience. "This time, I want to see seamless communication. Every move, every breath – I want to feel like we're one organism. Clear?"

A chorus of affirmatives answered him. Duggins allowed himself a small smile. They were good – damn good. But in this line of work, good wasn't enough. They needed to be perfect.

As the klaxon sounded, signaling the start of the next run, Duggins felt a familiar calm settle over him. This was where he belonged – in the thick of it, leading his team through the storm.

"Let's move," he commanded, and as one, they surged forward into the chaos of the simulated hostage scenario.

The klaxon's echo faded as Duggins led his team to the next phase of training. Sweat glistened on his brow as he surveyed the sprawling obstacle course before them. A labyrinth of challenges designed to push them to their limits.

"Listen up," Duggins barked, his piercing gaze sweeping across his team. "This course will test every skill you've honed. Treat it like a real op – your life and the lives of others depend on your performance."

He pointed to a towering wall, its surface deliberately rough and uneven. "You'll start there. Scale it, then navigate the tunnels. Watch for hostiles – they won't play nice."

As his team nodded in understanding, Duggins felt a familiar tightness in his chest. He'd designed this course himself, incorporating lessons learned from missions where split-second decisions meant the difference between life and death.

"Chen, you're up first," he ordered.

Chen approached the wall with determination etched on her face. As she began her ascent, Duggins watched intently, noting her technique.

"Good grip, Chen," he called out. "But watch your footing – an unstable perch could be fatal in the field."

Chen adjusted, her movements becoming more fluid. As she disappeared over the top, Duggins turned to the next team member.

"Ramirez, you're on deck. Remember, speed is crucial, but not at the expense of situational awareness."

Ramirez nodded, his jaw set. "Understood, sir."

As each team member tackled the course, Duggins provided constant feedback, his keen eye catching every misstep and moment of hesitation.

"Thompson, excellent use of cover in the tunnel section," he praised. "But your weapon transition was sloppy. In a real firefight, that could cost you."

Thompson's face flushed with a mix of pride and determination. "Won't happen again, sir."

Duggins nodded, allowing a hint of approval to show. "See that it doesn't."

As the last team member cleared the final obstacle, Duggins gathered them around. Despite their heaving chests and sweat-drenched uniforms, their eyes were alert, hungry for his assessment.

"Overall, solid performance," he began, his tone measured. "But 'solid' won't cut it where we're headed. Chen, your climbing technique is improving, but I need you faster on the descent. Ramirez, your tunnel navigation was textbook – keep that up."

He turned to Thompson. "Your marksmanship under pressure is impressive, but don't let it make you cocky. Overconfidence kills."

As he delivered his critiques, Duggins felt a swell of pride. They were taking it all in, already strategizing how to improve. This was why he pushed them so hard – because he knew they could take it, and because out there, anything less than perfection was unacceptable.

"We'll run it again in an hour," he announced. "Until then, hydrate and review your performance. I want to see significant improvements next round."

As the team dispersed, Duggins allowed himself a moment of reflection. How many times had he run similar courses? How many times had the skills honed here saved his life in the field? He shook off the memories, focusing on the present.

"They're getting better," he thought. "But will it be enough for what's coming?"

THE EXTRACTION

The sharp crack of gunfire shattered the air as Duggins stepped onto the firing range. His team was already in position, their focused expressions visible behind protective eyewear.

"Remember," Duggins called out, his voice cutting through the din, "speed is nothing without accuracy. I want to see tight groupings on those targets."

He watched as Jose Beals took aim, his movements fluid and precise. Three rapid shots rang out, all finding their mark within the bullseye. Duggins nodded approvingly, but noticed a slight tension in Jose's shoulders.

"Beals," he said, moving closer. "Your aim is spot on, but you're carrying tension. It'll slow you down in a real firefight."

Jose's jaw clenched. "Understood, sir," he replied, his voice tight.

Duggins frowned inwardly. Something was eating at Jose, but now wasn't the time to dig deeper. He made a mental note to address it later.

"Alright, team," Duggins announced. "Time to kick it up a notch. Multiple moving targets, varying distances. Go!"

The range erupted into controlled chaos. Bullets whizzed through the air, punctuated by the rhythmic pop of gunfire. Duggins observed his team's performance, his mind racing.

"We're good," he thought, "but good enough? What if Ali Shabaab has something unexpected planned? What if Raven Blackwood's intel is compromised?"

He pushed the doubts aside, focusing on the present. "Cease fire!" he called out. "Gear up for the next exercise. We're going dark."

Minutes later, Duggins led his team into a pitch-black, maze-like structure. The silence was oppressive, broken only by their controlled breathing.

"Remember," he whispered, "silent communication is key. One wrong move, one misplaced sound, and we're compromised."

As they moved through the darkness, Duggins felt a tap on his shoulder – their agreed-upon signal for a potential threat. He froze, straining his ears. A faint shuffle to their left. He signaled the team to hold position, then slowly advanced.

In that moment, navigating the unseen dangers, Duggins felt a familiar rush of adrenaline. This was where he thrived, where his years of experience translated into split-second decisions that could mean life or death.

"Stay sharp," he thought, his senses on high alert. "The real test is yet to come."

The fluorescent lights flickered to life, revealing a spartan training room with padded floors. Duggins stood at the center, his eyes scanning his team.

"Hand-to-hand combat," he announced, his voice echoing off the bare walls. "Pair up. Jose, you're with me."

Jose Beals stepped forward, a glint of challenge in his eyes. "Ready when you are, boss."

As the others squared off, Duggins and Jose circled each other. Duggins noted the younger man's taut muscles, the controlled aggression in his stance.

"Remember," Duggins said, "this isn't about winning. It's about—"

Jose lunged, a quick jab that Duggins barely dodged. "About staying alive," Jose finished, a hint of a smirk on his face.

They engaged, a flurry of punches and kicks. Duggins grunted as Jose's fist grazed his ribs. He retaliated with a sweep, sending Jose to the mat.

"Good," Duggins panted, offering a hand. "But watch your left guard."

As Jose regained his feet, Duggins caught sight of Ali Shabaab, methodically dismantling his opponent with precise, almost surgical strikes.

"Alright, switch!" Duggins called out. "New scenario. Hostage situation, abandoned warehouse. Ali, you're lead negotiator. Jose, you're the hostile."

Ali's eyebrows raised slightly, the only indication of his surprise. "Parameters?" he asked, his voice calm.

"Improvise," Duggins replied, studying Ali's reaction. "Let's see how you handle the unexpected."

As the team reset, Duggins couldn't shake a nagging feeling. Ali's composure was admirable, but was it masking something else? And Jose's aggression – an asset or a liability?

"Focus," he chided himself. "One challenge at a time."

Sweat dripped from Arthur Duggins' brow as he powered through his final set of deadlifts. The weight room echoed with grunts of exertion and the clang of metal. He glanced around, assessing his team's progress.

"Push it, people!" Duggins barked, his voice hoarse. "This isn't a day spa!"

Jose Beals was on the rowing machine, his face a mask of determination as he pulled the handle with explosive force. Each stroke seemed fueled by an inner fire, his jaw clenched tight.

"Beals," Duggins called out, "watch your form. Power from the legs, not just the arms."

Jose nodded curtly, adjusting his technique without breaking rhythm. Duggins noted the flash of frustration in the younger man's eyes. Always something to prove, that one.

Across the room, Virginia Turner was effortlessly gliding through a series of plyometric exercises, her movements precise and controlled. She caught Duggins' eye, a hint of a smirk playing at her lips.

"Impressed, Arthur?" she asked, barely out of breath.

Duggins grunted noncommittally. "Save your energy for the next phase, Turner. You'll need it."

As the team transitioned to cardio, Duggins' mind raced. The upcoming mission left no room for error. Every push-up, every sprint, every drop of sweat was a down payment on their survival.

Thirty grueling minutes later, Duggins led his sweat-soaked team to the outdoor range. The smell of gunpowder hung in the air as they geared up.

"Live-fire exercise," he announced, checking his weapon. "Multiple hostiles, civilians present. Engage on my mark."

Ali Shabaab methodically loaded his magazine, his expression unreadable. "Rules of engagement?"

"Shoot to neutralize," Duggins replied, studying Ali's reaction. "But watch your crossfire. We're not here to rack up collateral damage."

THE EXTRACTION

As they moved into position, adrenaline surged through Duggins' veins. This was where it all came together – strength, skill, and split-second decision-making.

"Go hot!" he yelled, and chaos erupted.

Targets popped up from behind barricades, some armed, some civilian. Duggins moved swiftly, his pistol an extension of his arm. Two shots, center mass, hostile down. A civilian target appeared; he held his fire.

"Contact left!" Jose shouted, his rifle chattering.

Duggins spun, engaging a flanking enemy. Out of the corner of his eye, he saw Virginia execute a perfect roll, coming up firing. Her shots found their mark with deadly precision.

As they advanced through the course, Duggins couldn't shake a gnawing doubt. His team was good – damn good – but would it be enough? The weight of command pressed down on him, heavier than any barbell.

"Clear!" Ali called out as they reached the final objective.

Duggins surveyed the scene, his breath coming in ragged gasps. "Good work, people. But remember, out there, we don't get second chances."

As they began to break down their gear, Duggins caught Jose staring at the targets, his knuckles white around his rifle. *What demons are you fighting, Beals?* he wondered. *And will they help us or hunt us when the bullets start flying for real?*

The team gathered in the dimly lit debriefing room, sweat still glistening on their brows. Duggins stood at the head of the table, his piercing gaze sweeping over each member.

"Alright, let's break it down," he began, his voice firm but not unkind. "Virginia, your marksmanship was spot-on, but I noticed a slight hesitation on that last civilian target. Split-second indecision can cost lives."

Virginia nodded, her jaw set. "Understood, sir. I'll work on quicker threat assessment."

Duggins turned to Ali. "Your situational awareness saved our asses when that surprise hostile popped up. Good work."

As he continued, providing targeted feedback to each team member, Duggins felt a familiar tightness in his chest. They're good, he thought, but good enough?

"Jose," Duggins said, locking eyes with the intense operative. "Your aggression is an asset, but I need you to dial it back 10%. We can't afford tunnel vision out there."

Jose's nostrils flared slightly, but he gave a curt nod. "Yes, sir."

After addressing the team's performance, Duggins leaned forward, his palms flat on the table. "Listen up. This isn't just about individual skills. It's about how we function as a unit. Our upcoming mission... it's not like anything we've faced before."

He paused, letting the weight of his words sink in. "The stakes are higher. The margin for error? Non-existent. But I've seen what each of you is capable of. Together, we're a force to be reckoned with."

Duggins straightened, his voice carrying a steely resolve. "We leave in 48 hours. Until then, I want you reviewing intel, fine-tuning your gear, and getting your heads in the game. Questions?"

Silence filled the room, broken only by the sound of determined breathing.

"Good," Duggins concluded. "Dismissed."

As the team filed out, Duggins remained, staring at the mission schematics on the wall. The faces of past operatives lost in the field flashed through his mind. Not this time, he vowed silently. Not on my watch.

As the room emptied, Duggins caught Jose's eye. "A word, Beals?"

Jose hesitated, then nodded, his jaw tightening. The two men waited until they were alone, the tension palpable.

Duggins leaned against the table, arms crossed. "I need to know we're solid, Jose. That aggression I mentioned - it's not just about the mission."

Jose's eyes flashed. "With all due respect, sir, if you have concerns about my performance-"

"This isn't about your performance," Duggins cut in, his voice low but firm. "It's about the chip on your shoulder. The one you've been carrying since Bogotá."

THE EXTRACTION

Jose flinched, a flicker of pain crossing his face. Duggins pressed on, "We can't afford divided loyalties or personal vendettas. Not where we're heading."

"My loyalty has never been in question," Jose growled.

"Maybe not. But your judgment has." Duggins stepped closer, his piercing gaze locked on Jose. "I need to know you can follow orders, even if they go against your instincts. Can you do that?"

For a moment, Jose said nothing, his internal struggle evident. Finally, he exhaled sharply. "Yes, sir. You have my word."

Duggins nodded, satisfied. "Good. Because I need you at your best, Beals. The team needs you."

As they moved to leave, klaxons suddenly blared throughout the facility. Red warning lights bathed the room in an eerie glow.

"What the hell?" Duggins muttered, already moving towards the door.

A voice crackled over the intercom: "All personnel, this is not a drill. We have a breach in Sector 7. Repeat, security breach in Sector 7."

Duggins and Jose exchanged a quick glance, years of training kicking in. Without a word, they sprinted down the corridor, their earlier tension forgotten in the face of an unexpected threat.

The cacophony of alarms filled the air as Duggins and Jose raced through the facility's corridors, their boots pounding against the polished floor. Duggins's mind raced, analyzing potential scenarios.

"Sector 7... that's the experimental weapons vault," he shouted to Jose over the din. "Could be Ali Shabaab's crew making a move."

Jose's face hardened. "Or worse, Raven Blackwood."

They rounded a corner, nearly colliding with the rest of their team converging from different directions. Duggins quickly assessed their readiness, noting the determined set of their jaws and the weapons already in hand.

"Listen up!" Duggins barked, his voice cutting through the chaos. "We're treating this as a hot situation. Unknown number of hostiles, potential high-value targets at risk. Standard breach and clear protocol. Questions?"

The team shook their heads in unison.

"Move out!"

As they approached Sector 7, the alarms abruptly cut out, plunging the facility into an eerie silence. Duggins held up a fist, bringing the team to a halt. He strained his ears, picking up faint sounds of movement beyond the reinforced doors.

"Something's not right," he thought, a chill running down his spine. "This feels too orchestrated."

Signaling to Jose, Duggins approached the security panel. As he reached for his access card, a sudden flash of movement caught his eye. He spun, raising his weapon, only to find himself face-to-face with a figure he'd hoped never to see again.

Raven Blackwood stood before them, a sardonic smile playing across their lips.

"Arthur Duggins," Raven purred, their voice a mix of silk and steel. "How kind of you to join us. I do hope I'm not interrupting anything important."

Duggins's finger tightened on the trigger, his mind racing. How had Blackwood infiltrated their most secure facility? And more importantly, what game were they playing?

"Stand down, Blackwood," Duggins growled, acutely aware of his team tensing behind him. "Whatever you're after, it's not worth it."

Raven's smile widened, a predatory gleam in their eyes. "Oh, I think you'll find it is, Arthur. In fact, I'm counting on it."

Before Duggins could respond, a deafening explosion rocked the facility, throwing them all off balance. As dust and debris rained down, Duggins caught a glimpse of Raven slipping away, their laughter echoing through the chaos.

"Secure the perimeter!" Duggins shouted, struggling to his feet. "Don't let them escape!"

But as his team scrambled to respond, a sinking feeling settled in Duggins's gut. Whatever Raven Blackwood had set in motion, he feared they were already too late to stop it.

CHAPTER 6

The acrid scent of burning rubber assaulted Arthur Duggins' nostrils as he stepped off the unmarked C-130, his boots sinking into the sun-baked tarmac of Baghdad International Airport. He squinted against the harsh midday glare, scanning the horizon where heat waves shimmered like mirages.

"Move out," Duggins ordered, his voice low and gravelly. The C.O.R.E. team fell in behind him, their movements fluid and synchronized after years of working together.

As they approached the bustling streets beyond the airport perimeter, Duggins felt the familiar tightening in his gut. Every shadow, every fleeting movement could conceal a threat. He pushed the thought aside, focusing on the mission at hand.

"Eyes sharp, people," he murmured into his comm. "We're in the lion's den now."

The team moved silently through narrow alleys, dust swirling around their feet with each step. Duggins' gaze darted from rooftop to doorway, cataloging potential sniper nests and ambush points.

A child's laughter echoed from a nearby courtyard, startling him. For a brief moment, Duggins allowed himself to remember why they were here – to protect the innocent from those who would do them harm.

"Sir," whispered Lopez, the team's comms specialist. "I'm picking up chatter on a known terrorist frequency."

Duggins nodded, his mind already racing through contingencies. "Can you pinpoint the source?"

"Negative, sir. Signal's bouncing off multiple relays."

"Keep monitoring. We need to know if our presence has been compromised."

As they rounded a corner, the streets opened up into a bustling marketplace. The cacophony of voices and smells momentarily overwhelmed Duggins' senses.

"Spread out," he commanded. "Blend in, but stay alert. These crowds are perfect cover for our rivals."

Duggins moved purposefully through the throng, his eyes constantly scanning faces and hands for signs of concealed weapons. A prickle at the base of his neck told him they were being watched.

THE EXTRACTION

"Johnson," he subvocalized into his comm. "I need eyes up high. Find us a perch with a good vantage point."

"Roger that, boss," came the sniper's calm reply.

As Duggins weaved through the market stalls, his mind raced. Were the rival groups already aware of their presence? Had they walked into a trap? The weight of command pressed down on him, each decision potentially spelling life or death for his team.

"Stay frosty," he reminded himself and his squad. "We've got a long way to go, and Baghdad's full of surprises."

The narrow alleyway loomed ahead, its shadowy depths promising both cover and danger. Duggins raised a fist, halting his team's advance. His eyes narrowed as he caught sight of movement at the far end.

"Armed tangos at twelve o'clock," he whispered, his voice barely audible over the distant market noise. "Checkpoint. Four... no, five hostiles."

Corporal Reyes crouched beside him, her rifle at the ready. "Rules of engagement, sir?"

Duggins' mind raced, weighing their options. The militants were positioned strategically, their weapons trained on the alley's entrance. Any frontal assault would be suicide.

"We can't risk alerting the entire neighborhood," he muttered, more to himself than his team. "Johnson, what's your status?"

The sniper's voice crackled in his ear. "In position, sir. I've got eyes on the checkpoint, but limited angle. Can't take them all out clean."

Duggins nodded, a plan forming. "Understood. Hold your fire until my signal."

He turned to his team, their faces a mixture of tension and determination. "We're going silent on this one. Hand signals only from here on out."

As Duggins began to outline their approach, a sudden burst of gunfire erupted from deeper in the city. The militants at the checkpoint tensed, their attention momentarily diverted.

"Now!" Duggins hissed, gesturing for his team to take cover behind the crumbling walls lining the alley.

THE EXTRACTION

As they pressed themselves against the sun-baked bricks, Duggins felt the familiar surge of adrenaline coursing through his veins. The weight of command settled on his shoulders, each decision carrying the potential for triumph or disaster.

'Just like Fallujah,' he thought grimly, pushing away memories of past missions gone wrong. 'Stay focused. Get it done.'

With practiced efficiency, Duggins began signaling his team into position. The plan was forming in his mind – a silent, coordinated strike that would neutralize the threat before the militants could raise the alarm.

As his team readied themselves, Duggins allowed himself a moment of grim reflection. How many more checkpoints, how many more firefights lay between them and their objective? Baghdad was a powder keg, and they were walking through it with a lit match.

"Steady," he whispered, more to himself than his squad. "We've got this."

Duggins' eyes narrowed as he scanned the checkpoint, his mind rapidly assessing each militant's position. With a series of quick, precise hand gestures, he assigned targets to his team members. A subtle nod here, a finger point there - each motion carried the weight of years of shared experience and trust.

'Johnson, take the one on the left. Martinez, the two by the vehicle. I'll handle the leader,' Duggins communicated silently, his fingers dancing through the air with practiced ease.

As his team acknowledged their assignments with barely perceptible nods, Duggins felt a familiar tightness in his chest. 'No room for error,' he reminded himself, pushing down the gnawing anxiety that threatened to surface.

The team began to move, their movements fluid and deliberate. Duggins watched as Johnson, his demolitions expert, slid like a shadow along the wall, positioning himself for a clear shot. Martinez, always reliable, was already in place, her steady hands gripping her silenced rifle.

Duggins inched forward, his boots barely disturbing the dust on the ground. Every muscle in his body was taut, ready to spring into action at a moment's notice. As he neared his position, a bead of sweat trickled down his temple, carrying with it the grit and tension of their mission.

'Just like we trained,' he thought, his mind flashing back to countless drills and simulations. 'But this time, it's for real. No second chances.'

With a final glance at his team, Duggins settled into position. The checkpoint loomed before them, oblivious to the deadly force poised to strike. In the eerie calm before action, Duggins allowed himself one last thought:

'Whatever happens next, we're committed now. God help us all.'

With a subtle nod from Duggins, hell broke loose. The team erupted into action, their movements a deadly choreography of precision and lethality.

"Go dark," Duggins whispered into his comm, his voice barely audible above the sudden burst of suppressed gunfire.

The militants at the checkpoint never stood a chance. Johnson's first shot caught the leader square in the chest, dropping him instantly. Martinez's rifle barked twice in quick succession, two more hostiles crumpling to the ground.

Duggins himself moved with fluid grace, years of training evident in every step. His sidearm, fitted with a suppressor, spoke softly but with devastating effect. Two more militants fell, their surprised expressions frozen on their faces.

'Clean and quick,' Duggins thought, his mind racing even as his body moved on autopilot. 'Just like we planned.'

The echoes of their muffled shots seemed to linger in the air, a haunting reminder of the violence that had just unfolded. Duggins scanned the area, his keen eyes searching for any signs of reinforcements or survivors.

"Status report," he hissed into his comm, his heart pounding in his ears.

"Clear," came Johnson's terse reply.

"All targets neutralized," Martinez added, her voice steady despite the adrenaline coursing through her veins.

Duggins allowed himself a moment of relief, but he knew better than to relax completely. In this hostile territory, danger lurked around every corner.

"Good work, team," he murmured, his eyes never leaving the alleyway entrance. "But stay frosty. We're not out of the woods yet."

Duggins moved swiftly, his experienced gaze sweeping the alley. "Martinez, Johnson, disposal. Quick and clean." His voice was barely above a whisper, but carried the weight of command.

As his team sprang into action, Duggins kept watch, every muscle taut with tension. The bodies were efficiently dragged into the shadows, stripped of anything useful. Within minutes, the alley looked undisturbed, as if the firefight had never happened.

"Sir," Johnson's voice crackled in his earpiece. "Area's clear. No trace left behind."

Duggins allowed himself a brief nod. "Regroup on me. Sixty seconds."

As his team assembled, Duggins felt the familiar surge of post-combat adrenaline. He looked at each of them, noting the glint of satisfaction in their eyes. They'd executed flawlessly, but he knew better than to let guard down.

"Good work," he murmured, his piercing gaze meeting each team member's eyes in turn. "But remember, we're still in hostile territory. Stay sharp."

Martinez nodded, her face a mask of concentration. "What's our next move, sir?"

Duggins paused, considering. The weight of command pressed on him, each decision potentially life or death. 'We've cleared this obstacle,' he thought, 'but how many more lie ahead?'

"We push forward," he finally said, his voice low but firm. "Our objective hasn't changed. This was just the first hurdle."

As they prepared to move out, Duggins felt a mix of pride and concern. They'd succeeded so far, but Baghdad was a labyrinth of dangers. He knew the real challenges were yet to come.

Duggins led his team through the winding alleyways, every shadow a potential threat. The acrid smell of gunpowder still clung to their clothes, a grim reminder of their recent encounter.

"Johnson, take point," Duggins ordered, his voice barely above a whisper. "Martinez, watch our six."

As they moved, Duggins's mind raced, analyzing every detail of their surroundings. 'The rival factions could be anywhere,' he thought, 'waiting to spring a trap.'

Suddenly, a metallic clang echoed from a nearby rooftop. Duggins raised his fist, signaling an immediate halt. The team froze, weapons at the ready.

"Sir," Johnson's voice crackled through the comms, "movement, two o'clock high."

Duggins's heart pounded, but his voice remained steady. "Hold position. Could be civilian. Could be hostile. Martinez, verify."

Martinez silently raised her scope, scanning the rooftops. After an agonizing moment, she reported, "Just a stray cat, sir. Area's clear."

Duggins exhaled slowly, the tension in his shoulders easing slightly. "Good catch, team. Let's keep moving."

As they resumed their advance, Thompson, the newest member, whispered, "Sir, how much further to the objective?"

Duggins considered his response carefully. "Far enough that we can't afford to let our guard down, Thompson. Every step could be our last if we're not vigilant."

The weight of his words hung in the air as they pressed on, each team member acutely aware of the dangers that lurked in every shadow, behind every corner. Duggins's mind raced with contingency plans, always preparing for the worst while hoping for the best.

'We've made it this far,' he thought grimly, 'but the real test is still to come.'

Duggins signaled the team to halt as they approached an intersection. The distant sound of voices drifted on the hot, dry air. He motioned for Jose to take point, knowing his second-in-command's keen instincts would serve them well.

Jose crouched low, inching forward to peer around the corner. His muscles tensed as he assessed the situation. After a moment, he retreated and whispered urgently, "Six hostiles, heavily armed. Looks like a patrol."

Duggins's mind raced through their options. "We can't engage," he muttered. "Too much noise. Ali, any alternatives?"

Ali Shabaab materialized beside them, his eyes gleaming with an unsettling intensity. "There is a passage through the old bazaar," he murmured. "It is treacherous, but it will conceal our presence."

Duggins locked eyes with Ali, searching for any hint of deception. The man's motives remained as inscrutable as ever, but they had little choice. "Lead the way," he ordered, "but remember, one false move..."

Ali nodded almost imperceptibly, a ghost of a smile playing on his lips.

As they slipped into the narrow alleyways of the bazaar, Duggins couldn't shake a growing sense of unease. 'Are we walking into another trap?' he wondered. 'Or is Ali genuinely helping us?'

The team moved silently through the shadows, the distant patrol fading behind them. Abandoned stalls and debris cluttered their path, forcing them to navigate carefully.

"Sir," Jose whispered, his voice tight with concern, "something feels off about this route."

Duggins nodded grimly. "Stay sharp. We're committed now, but be ready for anything."

As they rounded another corner, a figure suddenly loomed before them. Duggins's finger tightened on the trigger, but he held his fire as recognition dawned. A terrified merchant, caught in the wrong place at the wrong time.

"Please," the man whimpered in Arabic, "I mean no harm."

Duggins's mind raced. They couldn't risk the man raising an alarm, but eliminating a civilian was out of the question. He locked eyes with Jose, a silent understanding passing between them.

Duggins made a quick decision. "Jose, secure him. Quietly."

With practiced efficiency, Jose subdued the merchant, applying just enough pressure to render him unconscious without causing lasting harm. They dragged the limp body behind a stack of crates, concealing it from immediate view.

"We're leaving a trail," Emily muttered, her eyes darting nervously.

Duggins felt the weight of command bearing down on him. "Can't be helped. We push on."

As they resumed their trek, the distant wail of sirens pierced the air. Duggins's jaw clenched. "Double time," he ordered, his voice a harsh whisper.

The team picked up their pace, their boots nearly silent on the dusty ground. Ali led them through a maze of increasingly narrow passages, the walls seeming to close in around them.

'This better not be a dead end,' Duggins thought, his hand never leaving his weapon.

Rounding another corner, they came face to face with a high wall. Ali gestured urgently towards a small, inconspicuous door.

"Through here," he hissed. "It leads to the underground tunnels."

Duggins hesitated, eyeing the door suspiciously. "You first," he commanded Ali.

As Ali reached for the handle, a burst of gunfire erupted from behind them. Bullets ricocheted off the walls, showering them with debris.

"Contact rear!" shouted Mike, spinning to return fire.

Duggins's mind raced. "Emily, breach that door! Everyone else, suppressing fire!"

CHAPTER 7

The hinges creaked as Arthur Duggins eased open the safehouse door, his eyes adjusting to the dim interior. Stale air and the faint scent of mildew assaulted his nostrils. Cracked plaster walls and threadbare furniture spoke of neglect, matching the dilapidated neighborhood outside.

Duggins' gaze swept methodically across the room, muscles taut, ready to react. His mind raced through potential threats: hidden assailants, explosive devices, surveillance equipment. Nothing obvious, but in this line of work, obvious usually meant dead.

A floorboard groaned. Duggins' hand twitched instinctively towards his sidearm.

From the murky recesses of the room, a figure materialized. Middle-aged, with a face etched by time and hardship. The local informant. His eyes darted frantically, reminding Duggins of a cornered animal.

"You're late," the man hissed, his accent thick.

Duggins kept his voice low, steady. "Necessary precautions. We weren't followed."

The informant's gaze flicked towards the boarded-up windows. "You sure about that?"

Is he truly this paranoid, or is there something he's not telling me? Duggins wondered, studying the man's body language. Years of experience had taught him to read between the lines, to spot the telltale signs of deception or genuine fear.

"I'm sure," Duggins replied firmly. "Now, let's get down to business. You said you had critical information."

The informant's shoulders hunched, his voice barely above a whisper. "It's worse than we thought. The reach of Ali-Shabaab... it extends further than anyone realizes."

Duggins leaned in, his senses on high alert. "Explain."

As the informant began to speak, Duggins' mind raced, analyzing every word, every gesture. The stakes were too high for assumptions or mistakes. Whatever came next would shape the course of their mission – and potentially, the fate of countless lives.

Duggins took a calculated step forward, his hand casually resting on the holstered weapon at his hip. The cool metal against his palm was a reassuring presence as he sized up the nervous informant.

With a curt nod, he introduced himself. "Duggins. C.O.R.E."

The informant's eyes widened slightly, darting between Duggins' face and his hand on the weapon. Sweat beaded on the man's weathered brow.

"You... you're the one they sent?" the informant stammered, his voice barely above a whisper.

Duggins maintained his stoic expression, years of training kicking in. Don't show weakness. Don't give anything away. He mentally cataloged every twitch and nervous glance from the informant.

"I am," Duggins replied, his tone measured. "You have information for us?"

The informant hesitated, his hand hovering near his jacket pocket. Duggins tensed, ready to draw his weapon if necessary. *Is this a trap?* he wondered, his mind racing through potential scenarios.

After a moment that felt like an eternity, the informant slowly withdrew a folded piece of paper. His hands trembled as he held it out.

"This... this contains information about Ali-Shabaab's recent movements," the man explained, his voice quavering. "But it's coded. For your eyes only."

Duggins reached for the paper, his fingers brushing against the informant's clammy hand. As he took hold of the document, he locked eyes with the man.

"Tell me everything you know," Duggins commanded, his voice low and intense. "Every detail matters."

The weight of the situation pressed down on him. Whatever was on this paper could change everything. And judging by the informant's nervousness, it wasn't going to be good news.

Duggins unfolded the paper, his eyes scanning the series of intricate symbols. His brow furrowed as he focused, years of cryptanalysis training kicking in. Triangles, circles, and lines danced before him, a complex puzzle begging to be solved.

"These coordinates," he muttered, more to himself than the informant. "They're using a modified Caesar cipher."

The informant shifted nervously, glancing towards the boarded-up windows. "Can you make sense of it?"

Duggins didn't respond immediately, his mind working furiously to decipher the code. Patterns emerged, revealing potential locations, dates, and operational details. Each decoded fragment sent a chill down his spine.

"This is bigger than we thought," Duggins finally said, his voice tight. He looked up at the informant, studying the man's face. "How did you come by this information?"

The informant swallowed hard, his Adam's apple bobbing. "I have... connections. But that's not important now. What matters is—"

"Double agents," Duggins interrupted, his instincts flaring. "Within military intelligence."

The informant's eyes widened. "How did you—"

"It's all here," Duggins tapped the paper. "But I need to hear it from you. What do you know?"

The informant's shoulders sagged, as if a great weight had settled upon them. "They're everywhere," he whispered. "Working against you, against your mission. I've seen things, heard things..."

Duggins' mind raced. If true, this changed everything. Trust no one, a voice in his head warned. He clenched his jaw, realizing the magnitude of what lay ahead.

Duggins leaned in closer, his piercing eyes locked on the informant. "Tell me more about these double agents. What exactly are they after?"

The informant's voice dropped to a hushed whisper, his words laced with fear. "They're not just trying to stop you. They want Ali-Shabaab for themselves. Alive."

Duggins' brow furrowed, his mind racing through the implications. "For what purpose?" he pressed, his tone low and measured.

"Information, leverage, who knows?" The informant shrugged, his eyes darting nervously around the room. "But they're willing to sabotage your entire operation to get him."

Duggins felt his muscles tense, years of training kicking in as he processed this new threat. He needed more. Concrete details, something he could act on.

"I need specifics," Duggins said, his voice taking on a sharp edge. "Names, dates, anything that can corroborate what you're telling me."

The informant hesitated, and Duggins noticed a bead of sweat forming on his brow. Was it fear or deception?

"I-I don't have names," the informant stammered. "But there was a meeting, two nights ago. I overheard them discussing a plan to intercept your team near the border."

Duggins' eyes narrowed. "Where exactly?"

As the informant fumbled for an answer, Duggins studied him intently, searching for any tell-tale signs of lying. His instincts screamed caution, but he couldn't afford to dismiss this information outright. The stakes were too high.

The informant's hand moved to his sleeve, fingers trembling as he gripped the fabric. Duggins tensed, his own hand inching closer to his holstered weapon. With a swift motion, the man rolled up his sleeve, revealing a jagged scar running the length of his forearm.

"This," he said, voice barely above a whisper, "is what happens when you cross them."

Duggins leaned in, his keen eyes examining the mark. It wasn't a clean cut – the edges were rough, irregular. This wasn't the work of a surgeon or a careful torturer. This was brutal, hasty.

"When?" Duggins asked, his tone clipped but tinged with a newfound respect for the man before him.

"Three months ago. They caught me passing information to your agency. I barely escaped with my life."

Duggins' mind raced, correlating dates and events. Three months ago, they'd had a sudden dry spell in local intel. It all started to make a sickening kind of sense.

"Christ," Duggins muttered, more to himself than the informant. He straightened up, his posture shifting as the weight of this new reality settled on his shoulders. The game had changed, and he needed to adapt fast.

"Tell me everything you remember about that night," Duggins said, his voice low and urgent. "Every detail, no matter how small."

As the informant began to speak, Duggins listened with rapt attention, his analytical mind already formulating contingencies. They'd have to move carefully now, trust no one outside his immediate team. The mission had just become exponentially more dangerous, but also more critical than ever.

Duggins placed a firm hand on the informant's shoulder, his touch conveying both gratitude and reassurance. "Your information is invaluable," he said, his voice low and steady. "I give you my word, we'll do everything in our power to keep you safe."

The informant's tense shoulders relaxed slightly, but his eyes remained alert. "How can you be sure? These people, they have eyes everywhere."

Duggins' jaw tightened, his mind already cycling through extraction protocols. "We have safe houses that even our own agency doesn't know about. I'll personally oversee your relocation."

As he spoke, Duggins' hand instinctively moved to his comm device, ready to initiate the necessary protocols. But he paused, a flicker of doubt crossing his features. Who could he trust with this information? The pool of reliable allies had just shrunk dramatically.

"What about my family?" the informant asked, his voice barely above a whisper.

Duggins met his gaze squarely. "They'll be protected too. You have my word."

The two men locked eyes, a moment of understanding passing between them. Duggins saw in the informant's weathered face a mirror of his own determination, the same fire that had driven him through countless missions.

"We're in this together now," Duggins said, his tone brooking no argument. "The stakes are higher than ever, but so is our resolve. We'll uncover the truth, no matter the cost."

The informant nodded, a grim smile playing at the corners of his mouth. "Then let's get to work," he said, matching Duggins' intensity.

As they turned to leave the safehouse, Duggins felt a familiar surge of adrenaline. The mission had evolved, become more perilous, but also more crucial. He'd navigate these treacherous waters, root out the traitors, and see this through to the end. It's what he was trained for, what he lived for. And now, with this unlikely ally by his side, he felt more certain than ever that they would succeed.

CHAPTER 8

The moonless night cloaked the desolate stretch of desert in inky darkness. Arthur Duggins crouched behind a weathered boulder, his eyes scanning the horizon. A faint rustling caught his attention.

"Sandstorm," a voice whispered from the shadows.

Duggins' hand instinctively moved to his sidearm. "Clear skies," he replied, completing the coded exchange.

A lithe figure materialized beside him – Rashid, their local informant. Duggins studied the man's face, noting the tension in his eyes.

"The compound," Rashid murmured, unrolling a crude map. "Three layers of security. Outer perimeter patrolled every 15 minutes. Inner courtyard has motion sensors. Main building, reinforced steel doors, biometric locks."

Duggins absorbed the information, his mind already formulating strategies. "Guards?"

"Twelve on rotation. Armed with AK-47s and night vision."

"Extraction point?"

Rashid pointed to a spot on the map. "Here. But be warned, they have a new system installed last week."

Duggins nodded, committing every detail to memory. He tapped his comm. "Team, rendezvous at my position."

Within moments, four shadows converged on their location. Duggins surveyed his team, each member hand-picked for their unique skills.

"Alright, people," he began, his voice low but authoritative. "We've got our intel. Now let's break it down."

He turned to a stocky woman with close-cropped hair. "Martinez, you're on tech. I need those sensors disabled without raising alarms."

Martinez nodded, her fingers already dancing over her tablet. "I'll ghost their system. They won't know we're there until we're gone."

"Good." Duggins shifted his attention to a lean, wiry man. "Cooper, you're our eyes. Find us a blind spot in their patrol pattern."

"Consider it done, boss," Cooper replied, adjusting his scope.

Duggins continued, assigning roles with practiced efficiency. Each team member acknowledged their task, the gravity of the mission reflected in their focused expressions.

As he spoke, Duggins felt the familiar tightening in his chest – the weight of command, of lives in his hands. He pushed the feeling aside, concentrating on the objective.

"Remember," he concluded, his piercing gaze sweeping over the team, "we're here for Ali-Shabaab. In and out, clean and quiet. Any complications, we abort. Questions?"

Silence met his query. Duggins nodded, satisfied. "Move out in five. And watch your six – I've got a feeling this won't be a cakewalk."

As the team dispersed to make final preparations, Duggins found himself alone with his thoughts. The stakes were high, the margin for error non-existent. But this was what he was trained for, what he lived for.

He took a deep breath, centering himself. The calm before the storm settled over him, a familiar companion. Whatever lay ahead, Duggins knew one thing for certain – failure was not an option.

The night air hung heavy with tension as Duggins led his team towards the compound. Crouched low, he signaled with a gloved hand, directing their movement through the shadows. His eyes, sharp and alert, scanned the perimeter constantly.

"Patrol, two o'clock," he whispered, his voice barely audible.

The team froze, melting into the darkness. Duggins held his breath, counting the seconds as the enemy guard passed by, oblivious to their presence. Only when the footsteps faded did he release a silent exhale.

We're cutting it close, he thought, his mind racing through contingencies. One slip and this whole operation goes sideways.

As they approached the outer fence, Duggins raised a closed fist, bringing the team to a halt. Before them loomed a formidable gate, its electronic lock glowing ominously in the darkness.

"Cooper," Duggins breathed, "what are we looking at?"

The tech specialist inched forward, his eyes narrowing behind specialized goggles. "High-end stuff, boss. Biometric scanner, probably tied into their main security grid."

Duggins frowned, the furrows in his brow deepening. "Options?"

"We could try to spoof it," Cooper suggested, "but that'll take time we don't have."

"And risk tripping every alarm in the place," Duggins muttered. He turned to his demolitions expert. "Martinez, what about..."

"Too loud," Martinez interrupted, shaking her head. "We'd light up the night sky."

Duggins felt the pressure mounting. Every second they lingered increased their chances of detection. He needed a solution, and fast.

"What if," he began slowly, an idea forming, "we create a diversion? Something to draw their attention while we..."

A sudden crackle of radio chatter from a nearby guard cut him off. Duggins tensed, his hand instinctively moving to his weapon.

"New plan," he whispered urgently. "We're going over. Cooper, jam their comms. Martinez, I need a hole in that fence. Silent as the grave. Move!"

As his team sprang into action, Duggins felt a familiar rush of adrenaline. This was the chaos he thrived in, the knife's edge between success and catastrophe. But deep down, a nagging doubt persisted.

Are we walking into a trap? he wondered, his eyes scanning the compound beyond. Or is this just another day at the office?

Only time would tell. For now, all that mattered was the mission. And Arthur Duggins was determined to see it through, come hell or high water.

Duggins crouched beside the compound's security control panel, his weathered fingers working deftly to remove the cover. Beside him, Cooper kept watch, her eyes scanning the perimeter through night-vision goggles.

"How's it looking, sir?" Cooper whispered, her voice barely audible.

Duggins didn't respond immediately, his focus entirely on the tangle of wires before him. After a moment, he exhaled slowly. "It's a Cerberus 7 system. Newer than intel suggested."

"Can you crack it?" Cooper asked, tension evident in her voice.

Duggins allowed himself a grim smile. "They haven't built a system I can't beat yet." His hands moved with practiced precision, bypassing alarms and rerouting camera feeds. "Martinez, status on the surveillance loop?"

"Ready to deploy on your mark, boss," came the reply through his earpiece.

Duggins nodded, mostly to himself. "Execute in three... two... one... Mark."

A soft beep confirmed the success of their digital infiltration. Duggins stood, his joints protesting silently after the prolonged crouch. "We're dark. Move in."

As the team advanced towards the entrance, Duggins tapped Ramirez on the shoulder. "You're with me. We'll clear the guards."

Ramirez nodded, his face a mask of concentration as he checked his silenced MP5. Duggins could see the younger operative's fingers trembling slightly - a mix of adrenaline and nerves.

THE EXTRACTION

"Steady," Duggins murmured. "Remember your training. Clean and quick."

They approached the two guards stationed at the entrance, using the shadows as cover. Duggins felt his heartbeat slow, entering that state of hyper-focus that had saved his life countless times before.

In a fluid motion, Duggins emerged from cover, his silenced pistol already lined up. Two soft pfft sounds broke the night's silence, and the guards crumpled without a sound.

"Clear," Duggins whispered, his eyes already scanning for additional threats.

As Ramirez moved to secure the bodies, Duggins allowed himself a moment of reflection. The ease with which he'd just ended two lives troubled him, as it always did. But there was no time for moral quandaries. The mission came first.

"Entrance secure," he reported to the team. "Move up. And stay frosty - this has been too easy so far."

The words left a bitter taste in his mouth. In Duggins' experience, "too easy" often preceded "catastrophically wrong." As the team assembled at the entrance, he pushed the thought aside. Whatever came next, they'd face it together.

As Duggins and Ramirez dragged the bodies into the shadows, the rest of the team slipped past, their movements fluid and purposeful. Duggins watched them disappear into the compound's murky interior, a mixture of pride and concern churning in his gut.

"Let's move," he whispered to Ramirez. "We need to catch up."

They advanced swiftly, hugging the walls and staying low. The compound's oppressive silence set Duggins' nerves on edge. Where were the patrols? The guards? Something wasn't right.

As they rounded a corner, they nearly collided with Chen, the team's tech specialist. Her face was a mask of frustration.

"Problem," she hissed, gesturing to a heavy metal door. "It's locked. Biometric scanner and a keypad. Way more advanced than our intel suggested."

Duggins examined the door, his mind racing. "Options?"

"We could try to hack it," Chen replied, "but it'll take time. Time we don't have."

Ramirez piped up, "What about the air ducts? I saw an access panel back there."

Duggins weighed the choices, acutely aware of each passing second. The longer they stayed, the higher the risk of discovery. But rushing could lead to mistakes – fatal ones.

"Chen, start on the hack," he decided. "Ramirez, check those ducts. If they're viable, we go that route. If not, we wait on Chen. Either way, we're getting through this door."

As the team sprang into action, Duggins couldn't shake the feeling that Ali Shabaab was just on the other side, waiting. What secrets did the enigmatic figure hold? And more importantly, what dangers?

"Come on, come on," he muttered, willing the universe to grant them a break. But in his line of work, Duggins knew better than to count on luck. Whatever came next, they'd face it head-on – just like always.

Ramirez's voice crackled through the comms. "Duggins, we're in luck. Duct's wide enough. It'll be a tight squeeze, but it'll get us past this door."

Duggins nodded, his jaw clenched. "Good work. Chen, abort the hack. We're going up and over."

The team moved swiftly, their practiced motions betraying no hint of the tension coursing through their veins. Duggins watched as Ramirez disappeared into the vent, followed by Chen. He'd go last, covering their six.

As he pulled himself into the cramped space, Duggins's mind raced. What would they find on the other side? Ali Shabaab's reputation preceded him – a man of shadows and secrets. Duggins had dealt with his fair share of enigmatic figures, but something about this one set his teeth on edge.

The team emerged on the other side, dropping silently to the floor. Duggins scanned the room, his trained eyes picking out every detail. That's when he saw him.

Ali Shabaab sat in the center of the room, surrounded by four armed guards. His piercing gaze locked onto Duggins, a hint of a smile playing at the corners of his mouth.

"Ah, Mr. Duggins," Shabaab's voice was smooth, almost pleasant. "I've been expecting you."

Duggins's hand tightened on his weapon. "Have you now?" he replied, his voice low and controlled. "Then I hope you won't mind coming with us. Nice and easy."

Shabaab's smile widened, but it didn't reach his eyes. "Of course. But first, perhaps we should address the matter of my... associates?"

The guards tensed, their fingers hovering near triggers. Duggins's mind raced, calculating odds, angles, risks. They needed Shabaab alive, but they couldn't afford a firefight. Not here, not now.

"Your call, Shabaab," Duggins said, his voice steel. "We walk out of here together, or things get messy. Your choice."

In a heartbeat, the room erupted into chaos. One of Shabaab's guards made a sudden move, and Duggins reacted instinctively. His silenced weapon coughed twice, and the guard crumpled.

"Take them down!" Duggins barked, diving for cover behind a nearby desk.

The air filled with the muffled pop of silenced gunfire as his team engaged. Duggins peered around the edge of the desk, squeezing off controlled bursts at the remaining guards. One went down, clutching his chest.

"Shabaab's making a run for it!" Johnson, his second-in-command, shouted.

Duggins's eyes snapped to the center of the room. Ali Shabaab was indeed on the move, ducking low and heading for a side door.

"I've got him," Duggins growled, launching himself from cover.

He tackled Shabaab just as the man reached for the door handle. They hit the ground hard, Duggins using his weight to pin the target.

"It seems," Shabaab wheezed, "that your reputation for efficiency is well-earned, Mr. Duggins."

Duggins ignored the comment, quickly zip-tying Shabaab's hands behind his back. "Target secured," he called out to his team. "Status?"

"All hostiles neutralized," Johnson reported. "Minimal noise, sir. Don't think we've been made yet."

Duggins hauled Shabaab to his feet, studying the man's face. Despite the situation, Shabaab appeared unnervingly calm.

"You seem rather composed for a man in your position," Duggins observed, a hint of suspicion in his voice.

Shabaab's lips quirked into a half-smile. "Perhaps I simply understand the... fluidity of such situations, Mr. Duggins. Today's captor can be tomorrow's ally, after all."

"Save it for the interrogators," Duggins growled, shoving Shabaab towards the exit. "Johnson, take point. Torres, bring up the rear. Let's move, people. Extraction in five."

As they made their way out, Duggins couldn't shake an uneasy feeling. Shabaab's words echoed in his mind. What game was this man playing? And more importantly, were they walking into a trap?

Duggins led the team through dimly lit corridors, his senses on high alert. Every shadow seemed to conceal a potential threat. The weight of Shabaab's presence at his side only heightened his unease.

"Hold," he whispered, raising a fist. The team froze instantly.

Footsteps echoed from around the corner. Duggins' mind raced, calculating their options. They were exposed, caught between their objective and the exit.

"Jose," he breathed, barely audible. "Alternative route?"

Beals nodded, his eyes darting to a nearby air vent. "Tight squeeze, but it'll work."

Duggins made a split-second decision. "Do it. I'll create a distraction."

As the team hurriedly removed the vent cover, Duggins turned to Shabaab. "You're coming with me."

"A bold move, Mr. Duggins," Shabaab murmured, his eyes gleaming with interest. "But perhaps unwise."

Ignoring the taunt, Duggins pushed forward, rounding the corner with Shabaab in tow. They came face-to-face with a group of armed guards.

"Gentlemen," Duggins called out, forcing a casual tone. "I believe there's been a misunderstanding."

The guards raised their weapons, shouting in a mix of languages. Duggins' mind raced, searching for a way out that wouldn't compromise the mission or his team.

"Ali," he hissed, "if you value your life, you'll play along."

Shabaab's response was cool and measured. "And if I don't, Arthur?"

The use of his first name sent a chill down Duggins' spine. How much did this man know? And more importantly, what was his endgame?

The guards advanced, their weapons trained on Duggins and Shabaab. Duggins' hand inched towards his concealed sidearm, his muscles taut with anticipation.

Suddenly, a deafening explosion rocked the compound. Duggins seized the moment of confusion, drawing his weapon and firing in one fluid motion. Two guards dropped before the others could react.

"Now!" Duggins roared, diving for cover behind a concrete pillar.

His team burst from their hiding spot, unleashing a coordinated barrage of suppressing fire. The air filled with the acrid smell of gunpowder and the deafening staccato of automatic weapons.

"Impressive coordination," Shabaab remarked coolly, crouching beside Duggins. "Your team is well-trained."

Duggins glanced at him, suspicious of the calm demeanor. "Just stay down and don't do anything stupid."

He popped out of cover, taking down another guard with a precise headshot. His mind raced, analyzing the battlefield. They were outnumbered, but the element of surprise had given them an edge.

"Beals! Flank left!" Duggins ordered, his voice cutting through the chaos.

As Beals maneuvered, Duggins caught a flash of movement in his peripheral vision. A guard had circled around, taking aim at his exposed teammate.

Time slowed. Duggins knew he couldn't get a clear shot in time. His heart pounded as he prepared to witness the unthinkable.

Suddenly, Shabaab moved. With startling speed, he disarmed the guard and incapacitated him with a series of precise strikes.

Duggins stared, momentarily stunned. "Why did you-"

"Perhaps," Shabaab interrupted, his eyes gleaming with that same inscrutable intensity, "we share more common interests than you realize, Mr. Duggins."

Before Duggins could process this, the firefight intensified. He pushed the questions aside, focusing on the immediate threat. With renewed determination, he signaled his team to press forward.

"We're almost clear," he shouted. "Push through to the exit!"

As they fought their way towards freedom, Duggins couldn't shake the feeling that this mission had just become far more complicated than he'd ever anticipated.

CHAPTER 9

The night cloaked the compound in darkness as Arthur Duggins pressed his back against the cold concrete wall. He held up a fist, signaling his team to halt. Ahead, a guard's cigarette ember glowed, a pinprick of light in the gloom.

"Sierra Two, take him," Duggins whispered into his comms.

A muffled thud, then silence. Duggins nodded, satisfaction mingling with the ever-present tension coiling in his gut. One step closer to their objective. One step closer to Ali-Shabaab.

As they crept forward, Duggins' mind raced. How many more guards? Where exactly was their target being held? He pushed the questions aside, focusing on each careful footfall.

A door creaked open to their left. Duggins froze, muscles taut as piano wire. Two armed men emerged, speaking in low tones.

"... shipment arrives tomorrow. The boss wants..."

Duggins locked eyes with his second-in-command, Jake. A slight nod was all it took. They moved in perfect sync, years of training evident in every fluid motion.

Duggins struck like a viper, his knife finding the guard's throat before the man could cry out. Beside him, Jake dispatched the second guard with equal efficiency.

As they dragged the bodies into the shadows, Duggins murmured, "Good work. But we're running out of places to hide these guys."

Jake grunted in agreement. "Compound's crawling with 'em. Intel underestimated their numbers."

Duggins frowned. "Wouldn't be the first time. Stay sharp."

They pressed on, navigating the labyrinthine corridors. Each turn brought new dangers, new decisions. Duggins' instincts screamed at him to move faster, to find Ali-Shabaab before their luck ran out. But caution kept him in check. One misstep could doom them all.

A burst of automatic gunfire shattered the silence. Duggins cursed under his breath. "Foxtrot team, report!"

Static crackled in his ear, then: "Contact, east wing! Multiple hostiles!"

"Hold position," Duggins ordered. "We're coming to you."

As they raced towards the gunfire, Duggins' mind whirred. Had they been compromised? Was this a trap? Or had Ali-Shabaab orchestrated this chaos?

They rounded a corner and found themselves face-to-face with three heavily armed guards. Time seemed to slow as adrenaline surged through Duggins' veins.

"Down!" he roared, dropping to one knee as he opened fire.

The air filled with the deafening staccato of gunshots and the acrid smell of cordite. Duggins moved on instinct, years of training taking over. A guard went down, then another. The third managed to squeeze off a shot that grazed Duggins' arm before Jake took him out.

As the echo of gunfire faded, Duggins pressed a hand to his bleeding arm. "You good?" he asked Jake, voice tight with controlled pain.

Jake nodded, eyes scanning for more threats. "Yeah. You?"

"I'll live," Duggins grunted. "Come on. We need to regroup and find Ali-Shabaab before this whole operation goes to hell."

They moved forward, the sounds of distant combat spurring them on. Duggins' determination hardened. They would complete this mission, no matter the cost. Ali-Shabaab was here, somewhere in this maze of violence and secrets. And Duggins would find him.

As they regrouped with the rest of the team, Duggins couldn't shake the unease crawling up his spine. He scanned the faces of his operatives, searching for any sign of betrayal.

"Status report," he barked, eyes narrowing as Agent Reeves hesitated before responding.

"All clear on the west side, sir," Reeves said, avoiding direct eye contact.

Duggins' jaw clenched. "And the intel on Ali-Shabaab's location?"

"Nothing concrete yet," Agent Chen interjected, her voice a touch too eager. "But we've narrowed it down to the upper levels."

As Chen spoke, Duggins caught a furtive glance between her and Reeves. His instincts screamed danger.

"Alright, we're splitting up," Duggins announced, his tone brooking no argument. "Chen, Reeves, Rodriguez - you take the east wing. The rest of you, with me. We're heading up."

As the team separated, Duggins led his group towards the stairwell. His mind raced, analyzing every interaction, every subtle gesture he'd observed.

"Keep your eyes open," he murmured to Jake as they ascended. "Something's not right here."

Jake nodded, his grip tightening on his weapon. "You think we've got a mole?"

Duggins' lips thinned. "I think we need to find Ali-Shabaab before anyone else does."

They reached the upper floor, the tension palpable. Duggins motioned for silence, straining to hear any sign of their target. As they moved down the corridor, a whispered conversation drifted from around the corner.

"...can't risk it. If Duggins finds out-"

The voice cut off abruptly as Duggins rounded the corner, weapon raised. Two of his team members, Cortez and Walsh, sprang apart, guilt written across their faces.

"Find out what, exactly?" Duggins demanded, his voice dangerously low.

The silence stretched, heavy with unspoken accusations and fear. In that moment, Duggins knew - the mission, and perhaps his very life, hung by a thread.

The tense standoff was shattered by a sudden burst of gunfire. Bullets peppered the wall behind them, forcing Duggins and his team to dive for cover.

"Contact!" Jake shouted, returning fire from behind a metal cabinet.

Duggins pressed his back against the wall, his mind racing. "Rival group," he growled, recognizing the distinctive chatter of AK-47s. "They've beaten us to the punch."

He peered around the corner, catching a glimpse of black-clad figures advancing down the hallway. Their movements were precise, professional - these weren't run-of-the-mill terrorists.

"Jake, covering fire! Cortez, Walsh, flank left!" Duggins barked, pushing aside his suspicions for the moment. The mission came first.

As Jake laid down suppressing fire, Duggins sprinted across the corridor, bullets whizzing past his ear. He slid into position behind an overturned desk, his breath coming in short bursts.

"Who the hell are these guys?" Jake yelled over the cacophony of gunfire.

Duggins gritted his teeth. "Doesn't matter. They're between us and our objective."

He popped up, squeezing off three rapid shots. One of the attackers went down, but two more took his place.

"We're pinned down!" Cortez called out, frustration evident in her voice.

Duggins' mind raced, analyzing angles and positions. "Walsh, smoke grenade! On my mark!"

As Walsh readied the grenade, Duggins couldn't shake the nagging feeling that this ambush was too well-timed. Had someone tipped off these rivals? His gaze flickered to Cortez and Walsh, doubt gnawing at him.

"Now!" he shouted, pushing the thoughts aside.

The corridor filled with thick smoke, providing the cover they needed. Duggins surged forward, trusting his training and instincts to guide him through the haze.

Meanwhile, in the east wing, Chen's voice crackled over the comm. "Duggins, we've got a situation here. Different group, heavily armed. We're pinned down in the server room."

Duggins cursed under his breath. "Hold position. We'll rendezvous as soon as we can."

As he advanced through the smoke, engaging targets with practiced precision, Duggins couldn't shake the feeling that they'd walked into a trap. The question was: who had set it?

Duggins pressed his back against the wall, his breath coming in controlled bursts as he surveyed the heavy metal door before them. The acrid smell of gunpowder hung in the air, a stark reminder of the firefight they'd just survived.

"This has to be it," he muttered, his piercing gaze scanning for any signs of traps. "Ali-Shabaab's likely behind this door."

Jake crouched beside him, prepping the breaching charges. "Ready when you are, boss."

Duggins' mind raced, weighing the risks. Was Ali-Shabaab truly a captive, or was this another layer of deception? He pushed the doubt aside, focusing on the immediate task.

"Set the charges," he ordered, his voice low and steady. "Walsh, Cortez, cover our six."

As Jake worked, Duggins turned to his team. "Once we're in, expect anything. Ali-Shabaab's presence doesn't guarantee his allegiance."

The team nodded, their faces grim with determination. Duggins felt a swell of pride, tempered by the weight of responsibility. These were his people, and he'd get them through this.

"Charges set," Jake whispered.

Duggins took a deep breath. "On my mark. Three, two, one—"

The explosion rocked the corridor, the door blasting inward in a shower of metal and concrete. Before the dust could settle, Duggins was moving, his weapon up and ready.

"Go, go, go!"

They poured into the room, and for a split second, Duggins thought they'd miscalculated. Then all hell broke loose.

Muzzle flashes erupted from multiple positions, the staccato of gunfire deafening in the enclosed space. Duggins dove for cover behind an overturned desk, his instincts screaming.

"Contact front!" he shouted, returning fire. "Multiple hostiles!"

The room was a maelstrom of bullets and shouted orders. Duggins caught glimpses of his team finding cover, their training kicking in despite the chaos.

As he reloaded, Duggins' mind raced. This wasn't just an ambush; it was a well-prepared trap. But for whom? His team, or Ali-Shabaab?

"Jake, left flank!" he called out, spotting an enemy trying to outmaneuver them.

Jake's precise shots dropped the assailant, but two more took his place.

Duggins gritted his teeth, the familiar calm of combat settling over him. "Push forward! We can't let them pin us down!"

As he moved from cover to cover, engaging targets with practiced efficiency, Duggins couldn't shake the feeling that they were missing something crucial. Where was Ali-Shabaab in all this?

The firefight intensified, every second stretching into an eternity of split-second decisions and near misses. Duggins knew they needed to end this fast, or risk being overwhelmed.

"Walsh, frag out!" he ordered, preparing to capitalize on the moment of chaos.

As the grenade detonated, Duggins surged forward, determined to break the stalemate and uncover the truth behind this deadly puzzle.

The smoke from Walsh's grenade hadn't even cleared when Duggins heard a sickening thud. He spun to see Jake crumple to the ground, a crimson stain blooming across his chest.

"Man down!" Duggins roared, his voice tight with rage and grief. He unleashed a barrage of suppressing fire, giving Walsh time to drag Jake behind cover.

Duggins' mind raced. We're losing ground. Losing people. He steeled himself, pushing down the ache of loss. There'd be time to mourn later.

"Walsh, how's Jake?" he called over his shoulder, eyes never leaving his sights.

"Gone, sir," came the choked reply.

Duggins felt the words like a physical blow. He'd known Jake since their first days of training. Now wasn't the time for sentiment, but Jake's absence left a palpable void.

"Light 'em up!" Duggins ordered, his voice carrying a newfound edge of fury. "No quarter!"

The team responded with renewed vigor, their fire becoming relentless. Duggins watched enemy combatants fall, his own shots finding their marks with deadly precision.

As the last hostile dropped, an eerie silence fell over the room. Duggins' ears rang in the sudden quiet.

"Clear!" came the calls from his remaining team members.

Duggins rose cautiously, scanning the carnage. "Sweep for survivors and intel. Be thorough."

His gaze fell on a figure huddled in the corner. Ali-Shabaab. The man they'd come for.

Approaching carefully, Duggins saw the blood seeping through Ali-Shabaab's shirt. "You're hit," he said, kneeling beside him.

Ali-Shabaab's piercing eyes met Duggins'. "An occupational hazard," he replied, his voice strained but steady.

Duggins called over his shoulder, "Medic! We need that kit, now!" Turning back to Ali-Shabaab, he asked, "Can you move?"

Ali-Shabaab nodded grimly. "I've endured worse. Your timing, however, could have been better."

Despite everything, Duggins felt a wry smile tug at his lips. "Next time we'll call ahead."

As Walsh arrived with the med kit, Duggins helped Ali-Shabaab into a more comfortable position. "This isn't exactly how I pictured our meeting," Duggins admitted, applying pressure to the wound.

Ali-Shabaab winced. "Life rarely follows our scripts, Agent Duggins. I trust you have an exit strategy?"

Duggins nodded, his mind already planning their next move. "We do. But first, we need to get you patched up. This compound's about to become very unfriendly."

As Walsh worked on Ali-Shabaab's injury, Duggins surveyed his team. The loss of Jake hung heavy in the air, but there was a steely determination in their eyes. They had a job to finish.

"Once he's stable, we move," Duggins ordered. "Every second counts now."

The hallway erupted in gunfire as Duggins and his team emerged, Ali-Shabaab supported between two operatives. Bullets ricocheted off the walls, sending chunks of concrete flying.

"Contact front!" Duggins shouted, dropping to one knee and returning fire. His mind raced, calculating angles and assessing threats. "Walsh, Reyes, get Ali-Shabaab to cover!"

As his team scrambled for protection, Duggins caught sight of masked figures advancing from both ends of the corridor. Their movements were too coordinated, too precise. These weren't the same guards they'd encountered earlier.

"Rival group," Duggins muttered, his suspicions confirmed. He tapped his comm. "Team, be advised. We've got professionals on our six."

"Copy that," came Reyes' terse reply. "What's the play, boss?"

Duggins' eyes darted around, searching for an advantage. "We push through. Leapfrog maneuver. I'll take point."

Without waiting for acknowledgment, Duggins burst from cover, laying down suppressing fire as he sprinted forward. The acrid smell of gunpowder filled his nostrils, adrenaline surging through his veins.

He slid behind a pillar, heart pounding. "Move!"

As his team advanced, Duggins couldn't shake the nagging feeling that something was off. The rival group's tactics were familiar, almost predictable. It was as if...

"They knew we were coming," he breathed, the realization hitting him like a punch to

the gut. A grenade clattered at his feet, interrupting his thoughts. With lightning reflexes, Duggins scooped it up and hurled it back down the hallway. The explosion rocked the building, buying them precious seconds.

"Extraction point's two floors down!" Duggins yelled over the chaos. "We need to—"

His words were cut short as a figure emerged from the smoke, engaging him in close combat. Duggins blocked a vicious knife strike, countering with a swift elbow to his attacker's solar plexus.

As they grappled, Duggins caught a glimpse of his team fighting their way forward. Ali-Shabaab stumbled, then regained his footing, determination etched on his face.

Duggins finally gained the upper hand, subduing his opponent with a chokehold. As the masked figure went limp, Duggins' mind raced. Who were these people? How did they know about the operation?

Shaking off his doubts, he rejoined his team. They had a mission to complete, and time was running out.

The extraction point loomed ahead, a beacon of hope amidst the chaos. Duggins ushered his team forward, scanning for threats. As they approached, a figure emerged from the shadows, blocking their path.

"Arthur Duggins," the man sneered, his voice dripping with contempt. "So predictable."

Duggins froze, recognition dawning. "Kazimir. You're behind this?"

The rival terrorist leader chuckled darkly. "Oh, it's much bigger than you realize. Your precious C.O.R.E. has been compromised from within."

Duggins' mind reeled. The suspicious glances, the whispered conversations – it all made sense now. "A double-cross," he muttered, his jaw clenching.

"Precisely," Kazimir gloated. "We've been pulling strings for months, manipulating your operations. And now, we'll eliminate C.O.R.E.'s finest."

Duggins' eyes narrowed, his voice low and dangerous. "Not if I have anything to say about it."

Without warning, Kazimir launched himself at Duggins, a blade glinting in his hand. Duggins sidestepped, barely avoiding the slash. He countered with a swift jab to Kazimir's ribs, earning a grunt of pain.

As they traded blows, Duggins' mind raced. How deep did this betrayal go? Who could he trust?

Kazimir feinted left, then drove his knee into Duggins' stomach. Winded, Duggins stumbled back, his ears ringing with Kazimir's taunts.

"You're finished, Duggins. C.O.R.E. is done."

Gritting his teeth, Duggins surged forward, channeling years of training and experience into every move. He had to end this – for his team, for the mission, for everything he believed in.

Duggins' fist connected with Kazimir's jaw, the satisfying crunch of bone reverberating through his knuckles. The terrorist leader staggered, momentarily dazed. Seizing the opportunity, Duggins swept Kazimir's legs, sending him crashing to the ground.

"It's over, Kazimir," Duggins growled, pinning his opponent down.

Kazimir spat blood, his eyes wild with fury. "You think this ends with me? We're everywhere, Duggins. In your comms, your intel—"

A swift strike silenced him permanently. Duggins rose, his breath ragged, surveying the compound. "Clear!" he shouted, motioning to his team. "Extraction point secured!"

As his operatives rushed forward, Duggins' mind raced. How deep did this infiltration go? Who could he trust now?

"Sir, vehicle's ready," his second-in-command reported, snapping Duggins back to the present.

THE EXTRACTION

"Move out," he ordered, his voice steady despite the turmoil within. "We're not out of this yet."

The team scrambled into the waiting transport, engines roaring to life. Duggins cast one last glance at the compound, a fortress that had nearly become their tomb.

As they sped away, Mira, their tech specialist, turned to Duggins. "What now, sir? If what he said is true—"

"We trust no one," Duggins interrupted, his jaw set. "Not until we can verify every single member of C.O.R.E. Our mission just got a lot more complicated."

The vehicle lurched as it hit rough terrain, mirroring the turbulent thoughts in Duggins' mind. They'd secured Ali-Shabaab, but at what cost? And what new dangers awaited them beyond the compound's walls?

CHAPTER 10

The deafening crack of gunfire split the air as Duggins dove behind a crumbling concrete barrier, his heart pounding in his ears. Bullets peppered the ground around him, kicking up plumes of dust and debris.

"Jose, what the hell are you doing?" Duggins shouted, his voice barely audible over the chaos. He risked a glance over the barrier, spotting Jose crouched behind an overturned vehicle, his weapon trained on Duggins' position.

An explosion rocked the compound, showering them with fragments of twisted metal and shattered glass. Duggins' mind raced, struggling to process Jose's betrayal while assessing their dire situation. Ali-Shabaab huddled nearby, his piercing eyes locked on Duggins, silently demanding answers.

"Team, listen up!" Duggins barked into his comm. "Provide cover fire on my mark. We need to secure the package and get the hell out of here!"

As his team acknowledged the order, Duggins turned to Ali-Shabaab. "Stay close and do exactly as I say. Understood?"

The informant nodded, his face a mask of calm despite the mayhem surrounding them. Duggins couldn't help but admire the man's composure, even as doubt gnawed at him. Could he trust Ali-Shabaab any more than he could trust Jose?

"Now!" Duggins shouted, and a hail of suppressing fire erupted from his team's positions. He grabbed Ali-Shabaab's arm and sprinted across the open ground, bullets whizzing past their heads.

Thoughts raced through Duggins' mind as they ran. How long had Jose been planning this? What was his endgame? And most importantly, how would they complete the mission with their team fractured and their trust shattered?

As they reached the relative safety of a nearby building, Duggins pressed his back against the wall, his chest heaving. He locked eyes with Ali-Shabaab, searching for any sign of deception or fear. Finding none, he made a decision.

"We're getting you out of here," Duggins said firmly. "But when this is over, you and I are going to have a long talk about what the hell is really going on."

Ali-Shabaab's lips quirked in a humorless smile. "Assuming we survive, Agent Duggins, I look forward to it."

Another explosion rocked the compound, and Duggins steeled himself for the fight ahead. Trust or no trust, he had a job to do, and failure was not an option.

Duggins' instincts kicked in as he spotted movement in his peripheral vision. He spun, arm shooting out to catch the wrist of an enemy combatant lunging at him with a knife. In one fluid motion, Duggins twisted the attacker's arm and slammed him into the wall, disarming him with practiced efficiency.

"Stay close," he growled to Ali-Shabaab, his eyes scanning for more threats.

Two more hostiles emerged from the shadows, assault rifles raised. Duggins dropped low, sweeping the legs out from under the nearest attacker while simultaneously drawing his sidearm. A quick double-tap neutralized the second combatant before he could get a shot off.

"Impressive," Ali-Shabaab murmured, his calm demeanor a stark contrast to the chaos around them.

Duggins grunted, not taking his eyes off their surroundings. "Save the compliments. We're not out of this yet."

As they rounded a corner, a burst of gunfire erupted from their left. Duggins shoved Ali-Shabaab behind a stack of crates, returning fire and taking down another hostile.

"Duggins!" Jose's voice rang out, cutting through the din of battle. "Hand over Shabaab now, and we can end this!"

Anger flared in Duggins' chest. "What's your game, Jose? This isn't you!"

A sardonic laugh echoed off the compound walls. "You don't know me as well as you think, old friend."

More shots rang out, closer this time. Duggins' mind raced, trying to piece together Jose's motivations while formulating an escape plan. He glanced at Ali-Shabaab, who watched him with an unnerving intensity.

"Any insights you'd care to share?" Duggins asked the informant pointedly.

Ali-Shabaab's eyes narrowed. "Your colleague believes he's serving a greater purpose. He's gravely mistaken."

"And you?" Duggins pressed, ducking as another volley of bullets peppered their cover.

A ghost of a smile played on Ali-Shabaab's lips. "I am but a piece in a much larger game, Agent Duggins. One you've only begun to comprehend."

Duggins' jaw clenched as he processed Ali-Shabaab's cryptic response. He had no time to unravel the informant's riddles; survival was the priority now.

"Stay low," he growled, peering around the crates.

A flash of movement caught his eye. Jose appeared in his peripheral vision, gun raised. Duggins reacted instinctively, diving to the side as bullets tore through the air where he'd been standing.

"You're making a mistake, Jose!" Duggins shouted, returning fire.

Jose's voice carried a hint of desperation. "You don't understand what's at stake!"

Duggins' mind raced. What could have turned his trusted teammate against him? He pushed the thought aside, focusing on the immediate threat.

"Team, status report!" he barked into his comm.

Static crackled, then Martinez's voice came through. "Pinned down near the east entrance, sir. We're... we're not sure what to do."

Duggins could hear the confusion and fear in her voice. His team was fracturing under the weight of Jose's betrayal.

"Hold your positions and watch each other's backs," he ordered, trying to inject confidence into his tone. "We're all getting out of here."

A grenade sailed over their cover, forcing Duggins to grab Ali-Shabaab and roll away. The explosion sent debris raining down around them.

"Your team's loyalty is admirable," Ali-Shabaab remarked, brushing dust from his clothes. "But misplaced."

Duggins shot him a hard look. "Care to elaborate on that?"

Before Ali-Shabaab could respond, more gunfire erupted. Duggins spotted two of his team members, Chen and Rodriguez, caught in the crossfire, their faces etched with uncertainty.

"Chen! Rodriguez! On me!" Duggins shouted, providing covering fire.

As they scrambled towards him, Duggins saw the conflict in their eyes. Trust battled with doubt, years of camaraderie warring against the shock of betrayal.

"Sir," Chen began, his voice strained, "what's going on? Why is Jose—"

"I don't know," Duggins cut him off, "but right now, we focus on getting out alive. Questions later."

Duggins' mind raced as he assessed their precarious situation. The compound had become a war zone, with bullets whizzing past and explosions rocking the ground beneath their feet. He knew they couldn't stay here much longer.

"Listen up," he said, his voice low and urgent. "We're falling back to the extraction point. Chen, Rodriguez, you're on point. I've got Ali-Shabaab."

Ali-Shabaab's eyes narrowed. "And what guarantee do I have that you won't hand me over to your traitorous comrade?"

Duggins grabbed the informant's arm, his grip firm but not brutal. "Right now, I'm your best chance at survival. You want guarantees? Stay alive long enough to get them."

He tapped his comm again. "All units, fall back to extraction point Alpha. Establish a defensive perimeter and provide covering fire. Move!"

As his team acknowledged the order, Duggins turned to Ali-Shabaab. "Stay close and do exactly as I say. Understood?"

The informant nodded, his face a mask of calm despite the chaos around them.

Duggins took a deep breath, steadying himself. "Alright, let's move!"

They burst from cover, sprinting towards the compound's exit. Bullets peppered the ground at their feet, forcing them to zigzag unpredictably.

"Down!" Duggins shouted, tackling Ali-Shabaab as a rocket streaked overhead.

As they scrambled back to their feet, Duggins couldn't help but wonder if they'd make it out alive. But he pushed the doubt aside. He had a job to do, a team to lead, and an informant to protect. Failure wasn't an option.

Duggins and Ali-Shabaab rounded a corner, only to find Chen and Rodriguez hesitating, their weapons lowered.

"What's the holdup?" Duggins barked, his piercing eyes scanning for threats.

Chen shifted uneasily. "Sir, with all due respect... how do we know we can trust your orders after what happened with Jose?"

Duggins felt a twinge of frustration, but kept his voice steady. "We don't have time for this, soldier. The mission remains the same - extract the asset."

Rodriguez chimed in, "But sir, if Jose turned-"

"Enough!" Duggins snapped, his patience wearing thin. "You want to debate chain of command? Do it when we're not dodging bullets. Now move!"

As they pressed forward, Duggins' mind raced. He understood their doubts, but couldn't let it compromise the mission. Trust was a luxury they couldn't afford right now.

Suddenly, a metallic click echoed through the corridor. Duggins' instincts kicked in.

"Freeze!" he shouted, grabbing Ali-Shabaab's collar.

The floor in front of them erupted in a shower of shrapnel and debris. A pressure-plate mine.

"Damn it," Duggins muttered. "They've mined the compound. Eyes sharp, people. Watch your step and check every doorway."

As they navigated the treacherous hallway, Duggins couldn't shake a gnawing thought: How many more surprises did the enemy have in store? And could he keep his fractured team together long enough to overcome them?

Duggins pressed his back against the wall, sweat beading on his forehead as he peered around the corner. The compound's layout was a maze, but years of experience had honed his instincts.

"Two tangos, nine o'clock," he whispered, gesturing to his team. "Chen, pop smoke. Rodriguez, cover our six. We're taking the east corridor."

As Chen lobbed the smoke grenade, Duggins' mind raced. The extraction point was close, but the path ahead was uncertain. He had to keep his team focused, despite the lingering tension.

"Listen up," he said, his voice low but commanding. "I know you've got questions, but right now, we need to move as one. Trust in your training, trust in each other. We'll sort out the rest later."

The smoke billowed, obscuring their movement. Duggins led the way, his senses on high alert. Every shadow, every sound could be a potential threat.

Suddenly, a barrage of gunfire erupted from their right flank. Duggins cursed under his breath. "Contact right! Heavy weapons!"

The air filled with the deafening chatter of automatic weapons. Duggins could feel the tension radiating from his team as they returned fire.

"Sir," Rodriguez shouted over the din, "We're outnumbered!"

Duggins gritted his teeth, his mind racing through tactical options. "Fall back to the junction! We'll funnel them through the bottleneck!"

As they retreated, laying down suppressing fire, Duggins couldn't shake a nagging thought. How had the enemy known exactly where to hit them? The possibility of another mole gnawed at him, but he pushed it aside. Right now, survival was all that mattered.

"Chen, last claymore!" Duggins ordered. "Set it at the choke point. We'll buy ourselves some breathing room."

As Chen worked, Duggins assessed their dwindling ammunition. The extraction point was tantalizingly close, but with waves of hostiles between them and safety, he knew the real fight was just beginning.

The extraction point loomed ahead, a nondescript warehouse at the edge of the compound. Duggins and his team stumbled through the doorway, their breaths coming in ragged gasps. Ali-Shabaab, flanked by two operatives, was quickly ushered to the center of the room.

"Secure the perimeter," Duggins barked, his piercing eyes scanning for threats. "Rodriguez, get on comms. We need that evac bird here five minutes ago."

As the team scrambled to follow orders, Duggins allowed himself a moment to catch his breath. His muscles screamed from exertion, and the taste of copper lingered in his mouth. He spat, a streak of red staining the concrete floor.

"Status report," he demanded, his voice clipped and measured despite the chaos.

Chen limped over, favoring his left leg. "Two mags left, sir. Martinez took a hit to the shoulder, but he's mobile."

Duggins nodded, his mind racing through scenarios. "And Jose?"

A heavy silence fell over the room. Chen's eyes darkened. "No sign of him since the ambush, sir."

THE EXTRACTION

The weight of Jose's betrayal settled like a stone in Duggins' gut. He pushed the feeling aside, focusing on the mission at hand.

"Sir," Rodriguez called out, her voice tight with tension. "Evac's delayed. Heavy anti-aircraft fire in the area."

Duggins cursed under his breath. "How long?"

"Twenty minutes, minimum."

The team exchanged worried glances. Duggins could feel the fear and uncertainty radiating from them in waves.

"Listen up," he said, his voice carrying across the room. "I know we're all shaken. Jose's actions have put us all at risk. But right now, we need to focus on getting Ali-Shabaab out of here alive."

He locked eyes with each team member, conveying a mix of determination and empathy. "We've trained for this. We're the best of the best. And I need each of you to remember that now."

Martinez spoke up, his voice strained with pain. "How can we trust anyone after what Jose did?"

Duggins felt a surge of anger and betrayal, but he kept his voice steady. "We trust in our mission. We trust in our training. And most importantly, we trust in each other. Jose made his choice, but we still have a job to do."

He turned to Ali-Shabaab, who had remained eerily calm throughout the ordeal. "And you," Duggins said, his eyes narrowing. "I hope you understand the price we've paid to get you out. Whatever information you have better be worth it."

Ali-Shabaab met Duggins' gaze, his expression unreadable. "The attack on Tel Aviv is only the beginning," he said cryptically. "What I know will change everything."

Duggins felt a chill run down his spine. He opened his mouth to press further when the distinct sound of approaching vehicles cut through the air.

"Contact!" Chen shouted from his position by the window. "Multiple technicals, approaching fast!"

Duggins' mind raced. Twenty minutes until evac. Dwindling ammunition. A fractured team. And now, a new wave of hostiles closing in.

He took a deep breath, steadying himself. "Alright, people. This is where we earn our pay. Chen, Rodriguez - I want killzones established at those entrances. Martinez, you're on overwatch. Everyone else, find cover and conserve ammo. We hold this position no matter what."

As his team moved to their positions, Duggins allowed himself one last moment of doubt. Could he really trust anyone after Jose's betrayal? He pushed the thought aside. Right now, trust was all they had.

"Lock and load," he ordered, raising his rifle. "Let's show these bastards what we're made of."

Duggins scanned the room, his eyes landing on each member of his battered team. Despite their exhaustion, he saw a renewed determination in their faces. They'd been through hell, but they weren't broken.

"Listen up," he said, his voice low and intense. "I know we're all reeling from what happened back there. But right now, that doesn't matter. What matters is stopping that attack on Tel Aviv."

Martinez, her face streaked with dirt and sweat, spoke up. "How do we know there's even still a threat? Jose could've been lying about everything."

Duggins shook his head. "We can't take that chance. Too many lives are at stake."

He turned to Ali-Shabaab, who was huddled in the corner, eyes darting nervously. "You. Start talking. What exactly are we dealing with?"

As Ali-Shabaab opened his mouth to respond, the building shook with a nearby explosion. Dust rained down from the ceiling.

"Incoming!" Chen shouted from his position.

Duggins' mind raced, weighing options. They were pinned down, outnumbered, with dwindling resources. But giving up wasn't an option.

He made a quick decision. "Rodriguez, Chen - lay down suppressing fire. Martinez, I need you to get that sat-phone working. We need to call in air support."

As his team sprang into action, Duggins felt a grim resolve settle over him. They'd faced betrayal, ambushes, and seemingly insurmountable odds. But they were still standing. And as long as they were standing, they had a chance.

"Whatever it takes," he muttered to himself, checking his weapon. "We're stopping that attack."

CHAPTER 11

The acrid smell of gunpowder filled Ali Shabaab's nostrils as he crouched behind a crumbling wall, his heart pounding. Sweat trickled down his face, mingling with the dust that caked his skin. The distant wail of sirens pierced the night air.

"Move, now!" hissed a voice in his ear.

Ali's muscles tensed as he sprang into action, darting from cover to cover. His eyes scanned the shadows, searching for threats. The weight of the stolen documents pressed against his chest, a constant reminder of what was at stake.

As he rounded a corner, a figure emerged from the darkness. Ali's hand instinctively went to his weapon, but he relaxed when he recognized the face of his mentor, Zaid.

"Well done, my protégé," Zaid whispered, his eyes gleaming with pride. "You've proven yourself tonight."

Ali nodded, his chest swelling with a mixture of relief and accomplishment. "The intel was accurate. We got what we came for."

Zaid's hand clasped Ali's shoulder. "This is just the beginning. With your skills, we can reshape the world."

Ali's mind raced. Is this truly the path I want? he wondered. But the thrill of success, the newfound respect in Zaid's eyes, silenced his doubts.

"What's our next move?" Ali asked, his voice steady despite his inner turmoil.

Zaid's lips curled into a smile. "We have powerful friends waiting to meet you. Your actions tonight have opened many doors."

As they melted into the shadows, Ali felt the weight of his choices settling upon him. He had crossed a line, and there was no going back. The terrorist underworld had embraced him, and he found himself both exhilarated and terrified by the possibilities that lay ahead.

Ali's heart pounded as he crouched behind a crumbling wall, the acrid smell of gunpowder filling his nostrils. Zaid's voice crackled through his earpiece, "The target is approaching. Remember your training."

Ali's fingers tightened around his rifle. This wasn't just another operation; it was a test. His gaze fell on the approaching vehicle, knowing the passenger inside was a high-ranking government official – and his childhood friend.

As the car drew nearer, memories flooded Ali's mind. Laughter shared over soccer games, dreams whispered under starlit skies. Could he really do this?

"Now, Ali!" Zaid's voice commanded.

Time seemed to slow. Ali's finger hovered over the trigger, his breath caught in his throat. In that moment, he saw two paths stretching before him – one of unwavering loyalty, the other of devastating betrayal.

With a sharp intake of breath, Ali made his choice. The rifle clattered to the ground.

"I can't do it," he whispered, his voice breaking.

The scene dissolved, bringing Ali back to the present. He found himself seated across from Arthur Duggins, the C.O.R.E. team leader's piercing gaze fixed upon him.

"The attack will occur within 48 hours," Ali stated, his voice devoid of emotion. "They plan to target three locations simultaneously."

Duggins leaned forward, his eyes narrowing. "And how can we be certain this information is reliable?"

Ali's face remained impassive, betraying nothing of the turmoil within. "You can't," he replied simply. "But ask yourself, Agent Duggins, what do I have to gain by misleading you?"

A tense silence filled the room. Ali could almost see the gears turning in Duggins' mind, weighing the risks against the potential payoff.

Finally, Duggins spoke. "Very well. We'll act on this intelligence. But know this – if this turns out to be a trap, there won't be a hole deep enough for you to hide in."

Ali nodded, his expression unchanged. As Duggins left the room, Ali allowed himself a moment of reflection. The path that had led him here was fraught with impossible choices and bitter regrets. But as he thought of the lives that hung in the balance, he knew that this, at last, was the right decision.

Ali's stoic facade cracked for a moment as he watched Duggins leave. He closed his eyes, allowing himself to be pulled into another memory.

The dusty streets of Mogadishu materialized around him. A younger Ali stood in the shadows, watching a group of children play soccer with a makeshift ball. Among them was his younger brother, Farhan, his laughter echoing through the alley.

Suddenly, the scene erupted in chaos. An explosion rocked the street, debris raining down. When the dust settled, Ali found himself cradling Farhan's lifeless body, his brother's blood staining his hands.

"This is why," Ali whispered to himself, snapping back to the present. "This is why it must end."

The door burst open, startling Ali from his reverie. Arthur Duggins stormed in, his face a mask of barely contained frustration.

"Your intel doesn't add up," Duggins growled, slamming a file on the table. "We've cross-referenced it with our sources, and there are discrepancies."

Ali leaned forward, his piercing gaze meeting Duggins'. "Perhaps your sources are compromised," he suggested calmly.

Duggins' fist connected with the table. "Don't play games with me, Shabaab. Lives are at stake."

"I'm acutely aware of that fact, Agent Duggins," Ali replied, his voice ice-cold. "More than you know."

"Then start talking," Duggins demanded. "No more cryptic answers. No more half-truths."

Ali's mind raced, weighing the risks of revealing too much against the need to gain Duggins' trust. "Very well," he said finally. "But understand this – the information I'm about to share could get us both killed."

Duggins leaned back, his eyes never leaving Ali's face. "I'm listening."

The tension in the room was palpable as Ali prepared to speak, but before he could, the door swung open again. A figure stepped in, causing Ali's blood to run cold.

"Malik," Ali breathed, his composure momentarily shaken.

The newcomer's lips curled into a cruel smile. "Ali, my old friend. It's been too long."

Duggins' hand instinctively moved to his holster. "Who the hell are you?"

Malik ignored him, his eyes fixed on Ali. "Still playing both sides, I see. Some things never change."

Ali's mind raced, memories flooding back. Malik, once a brother-in-arms, now represented everything Ali had grown to despise about the terrorist underworld.

"What are you doing here, Malik?" Ali asked, his voice steady despite the turmoil within.

Malik circled the room, his presence predatory. "I could ask you the same question. Consorting with the enemy now, are we?"

Ali's fists clenched under the table. "The real enemy isn't who you think it is."

"Enlighten me," Malik sneered.

THE EXTRACTION

As Ali opened his mouth to respond, a vivid flashback seized him. He was back in Mogadishu, the acrid smell of smoke filling his nostrils. Gunfire erupted around him, and he saw his younger sister, Amira, caught in the crossfire.

"No!" Ali screamed, both in the memory and in the present.

Duggins and Malik both startled at his outburst.

Ali's voice cracked as he spoke, "This endless cycle of violence... it took everything from me. My brother, my sister... When does it end, Malik?"

Malik's expression softened for a moment before hardening again. "It ends when we achieve our goals, Ali. You used to understand that."

"And at what cost?" Ali challenged, his resolve strengthening. "How many more innocents must die?"

The room fell silent, the weight of Ali's words hanging in the air. Duggins watched the exchange, his suspicion of Ali warring with a newfound understanding.

Ali-Shabaab leaned forward, his fingers interlaced on the table. The harsh fluorescent light cast deep shadows across his face, accentuating the weariness in his eyes. Duggins stood at the far end of the room, arms crossed, his gaze boring into Ali.

"You expect us to trust you?" Duggins' voice was low, tinged with skepticism. "After everything you've done?"

Ali's jaw clenched, a flicker of frustration crossing his features. "I've given you actionable intelligence. What more do you want?"

"The truth," Duggins shot back. "Your whole truth."

Ali's fingers twitched, betraying his inner turmoil. "My truth?" he said, his voice barely above a whisper. "My truth is that I've seen enough bloodshed to last lifetimes."

He stood abruptly, pacing the small room. "You think I don't understand your suspicion? I've been where you are, Duggins. But right now, we don't have the luxury of mistrust."

Duggins' eyes narrowed. "Prove it. Give us something concrete, something we can verify."

THE EXTRACTION

Ali paused, closing his eyes as a memory washed over him. He was back in Gaza, the acrid smell of smoke and cordite filling his nostrils. Gunfire echoed in the distance as he crouched behind a crumbling wall, his heart pounding.

"Two years ago," Ali began, his voice hoarse. "I was part of an operation in Gaza. We were supposed to target a military installation, but our intel was flawed."

He turned to face Duggins, his eyes haunted. "It was a school, Duggins. A goddamn school full of children."

The room fell silent, the weight of Ali's words hanging heavy in the air.

"I couldn't do it," Ali continued, his voice barely above a whisper. "I sabotaged the operation, warned the school. But the damage was already done. The conflict escalated, and both sides paid the price in blood."

Duggins' stance softened slightly, but his eyes remained wary. "And now?"

Ali met his gaze unflinchingly. "Now, I have a chance to prevent another tragedy. Will you let me?"

Ali's eyes locked onto Duggins, a newfound intensity burning within them. "The attack is set for tomorrow at 0600. They're targeting the Israeli embassy in London."

Duggins' body tensed, his hand instinctively reaching for his comm device. "How certain are you?"

"Absolutely certain," Ali replied, his voice carrying a weight that silenced any lingering doubts. "They're using a new type of explosive, undetectable by standard security measures. It's already in place."

The room erupted into a flurry of activity. Duggins barked orders into his comm, his words clipped and urgent. "I need all hands on deck. Full lockdown of the embassy district. Now!"

Ali continued, his words coming faster now. "There's more. The bomb is just a diversion. The real target is a visiting dignitary - code name 'Olive Branch'. They plan to assassinate them during the chaos."

Duggins' eyes widened, the implications hitting him like a physical blow. "Christ," he muttered, running a hand through his hair. "If they succeed..."

"It would shatter any hope for peace talks," Ali finished grimly. "Decades of progress, gone in an instant."

As the team mobilized around them, Duggins turned back to Ali, his expression a mix of gratitude and lingering suspicion. "Why tell us this now? Why risk everything?"

Ali's gaze drifted, a flicker of something unreadable passing across his face. "Perhaps I'm tired of watching the world burn," he said softly. Then, meeting Duggins' eyes once more, he added, "Or perhaps I have my own agenda. Does it matter, as long as we stop this attack?"

Duggins hesitated, his instincts warring with the urgency of the situation. Finally, he nodded. "For now, no. But this isn't over, Ali. Not by a long shot."

As Duggins turned to leave, Ali called out, his voice carrying an edge that made the agent pause. "One last thing, Duggins. Watch for the white dove. It's not what you think."

Duggins spun around, questions forming on his lips, but Ali had already retreated into silence, his enigmatic warning hanging in the air like a challenge.

CHAPTER 12

The night exploded in a hail of gunfire. Arthur Duggins dove behind a crumbling wall, his heart pounding as bullets whizzed overhead.

"Contact front!" he shouted, his voice cutting through the chaos. "Delta team, suppressing fire left flank. Charlie, with me on the right."

Duggins' mind raced, analyzing the situation with practiced efficiency. Three... no, four enemy positions. Heavy weapons to the north. Limited cover between here and the extraction point.

He peered around the wall, eyes scanning for movement. A muzzle flash caught his attention.

"Sniper, second floor, blue building," Duggins barked into his comm. "Johnson, take him out."

The crack of a rifle answered, followed by silence from the building.

Good man, Johnson. Always on point.

Duggins motioned to his second-in-command. "Torres, what's our ammo situation?"

"Running low, sir. Maybe two mags each."

Damn. This was supposed to be a simple grab and go. How did they know we were coming?

"Sir, what's the play?" Torres asked, tension evident in his voice.

Duggins took a deep breath, centering himself. His team looked to him for direction, for hope. He couldn't let them down.

"We push through to the southeast alley," Duggins said, his tone firm and assured. "It's our best shot at breaking contact. Delta lays down cover fire while Charlie moves. Then we swap."

He locked eyes with each member of his team, seeing determination reflected back. They were ready.

"On my mark," Duggins said, gripping his weapon tightly. "Three, two, one... MOVE!"

The world erupted into chaos as Duggins and his team surged forward. Bullets whizzed past, their high-pitched whines a deadly symphony. The acrid smell of cordite filled the air, mixing with the dust kicked up by near misses.

"Contact left!" Torres shouted, his rifle chattering as he returned fire.

An explosion rocked the ground, showering them with debris. Duggins' ears rang, but he pushed through the disorientation.

"Keep moving!" he yelled, his voice hoarse. "Don't bunch up!"

As they advanced, Duggins caught sight of Ali-Shabaab, hunched behind a low wall. The man's eyes were wide, but his face remained impassive. For a brief moment, their gazes locked.

Time seemed to slow as a realization hit Duggins like a physical blow. The gravity of the situation crystallized in his mind. *We can't let them take Ali-Shabaab alive. The intel he carries... it could compromise everything.*

Duggins felt his throat tighten. The mission parameters were clear: extract the asset at all costs. But now, with enemy forces closing in, the calculus had changed.

He could end it now. One shot. Clean. Quick. It would ensure the safety of countless operatives in the field.

But as he raised his weapon, doubt crept in. This wasn't a faceless target. This was a man they'd been tasked to protect. A potential goldmine of information that could save lives.

"Duggins!" Johnson's voice crackled over the comm. "We're pinned down! What are your orders?"

The weight of command pressed down on him. His team was counting on him. The mission was hanging by a thread. And time was running out.

Duggins swallowed hard, his finger hovering over the trigger as he stared at Ali-Shabaab. The man's eyes never wavered, as if daring Duggins to make a choice.

"Sir?" Torres asked, urgency in his voice. "What's the call?"

Duggins' jaw clenched, his decision crystallizing in a heartbeat. "Protect the asset," he barked, lowering his weapon. "Form a perimeter around Ali-Shabaab. We're getting him out of here alive."

The team snapped into action, converging around their charge. Duggins caught a flicker of surprise in Ali-Shabaab's eyes before it vanished behind his usual mask of calm.

"Johnson, Torres, take point. Martinez, watch our six," Duggins ordered, his voice steady despite the chaos. "I've got the asset. Move!"

They surged forward, a well-oiled machine forged in the crucible of countless missions. Bullets whizzed past, kicking up dirt and splintering wood. Duggins felt the sting of shrapnel grazing his cheek but pushed the pain aside.

"Contact, ten o'clock!" Johnson shouted, dropping to one knee and returning fire.

Duggins grabbed Ali-Shabaab's arm, pulling him down behind a crumbling wall. "Stay low," he growled, scanning for threats.

The air was thick with gunsmoke and the acrid smell of cordite. Duggins' heart pounded, adrenaline surging through his veins. *Did I make the right call?* The doubt gnawed at him, but he shoved it aside. No time for second-guessing now.

"Grenade!" Martinez's warning pierced the cacophony.

Without hesitation, Duggins threw himself over Ali-Shabaab, shielding him with his body as the explosion rocked the ground. Debris rained down, and for a moment, the world went silent except for the ringing in his ears.

As the dust settled, Duggins locked eyes with Ali-Shabaab. The man's expression was unreadable, but there was a glimmer of... something. Respect? Calculation? Duggins couldn't be sure.

"You didn't have to do that," Ali-Shabaab said softly.

Duggins grunted, hauling them both to their feet. "Part of the job description," he replied tersely. "Now move. We're not out of this yet."

"Covering fire!" Duggins barked, his voice cutting through the chaos. "Johnson, Martinez, suppress that sniper nest!"

The staccato burst of automatic weapons filled the air as his team responded instantly.

"Copy that!" Johnson's voice crackled through the comms.

Duggins grabbed Ali-Shabaab's collar, pushing him towards a narrow alleyway. "Move, now!" he commanded, his eyes scanning for threats.

Ali-Shabaab stumbled forward, his usual composure slipping. "Your men, they fight well," he muttered, a hint of admiration in his accented voice.

"Save your breath," Duggins growled, every nerve on high alert. We're not out of this hellhole yet.

A sudden movement caught Duggins' eye. "Down!" he roared, shoving Ali-Shabaab to the ground.

The world exploded into a maelstrom of noise and debris. Duggins felt the searing heat of a bullet passing inches from his face. Time seemed to slow as he turned, watching in horror as Ali-Shabaab's body jerked violently.

No, no, no! Duggins' mind raced. This can't be happening. The mission, everything we've worked for...

Ali-Shabaab's eyes widened in shock, his hand clutching at the rapidly spreading crimson stain on his chest. The usually stoic man's face contorted in pain and disbelief.

Duggins felt the blood drain from his face, his heart pounding in his ears. The consequences of his choices crashed down upon him like a tidal wave. Everything hinged on keeping Ali-Shabaab alive, and now...

"Man down!" Duggins shouted, his voice barely recognizable to his own ears. "Medic! We need immediate evac!"

As he applied pressure to Ali-Shabaab's wound, Duggins met the man's fading gaze. In that moment, he saw not an asset or a target, but a human being slipping away. And with him, the key to unraveling a web of international intrigue that could change the course of history.

Bullets whizzed past Duggins' head as he dragged Ali-Shabaab behind a crumbling wall. His muscles screamed in protest, every movement a battle against exhaustion and adrenaline.

"Beals! Cover fire, now!" Duggins barked, his voice hoarse from the acrid smoke filling the air.

Jose Beals unleashed a barrage of suppressing fire, his face a mask of grim determination. "Running low on ammo, boss!" he shouted between bursts.

Duggins' mind raced, assessing their dwindling options. *We're pinned down, outnumbered, and our primary asset is bleeding out. How the hell do we get out of this?*

He glanced at Ali-Shabaab, whose breathing had become shallow and labored. The man's eyes, once sharp and calculating, now held a glassy, distant look.

"Stay with me," Duggins growled, applying more pressure to the wound. "You don't get to check out yet, not after all this."

A nearby explosion showered them with debris, forcing Duggins to shield Ali-Shabaab's body with his own. The relentless assault was taking its toll, each impact reverberating through his battered body.

"Arthur," Jose's voice cut through the chaos, a hint of desperation creeping in. "We can't hold this position much longer."

Duggins nodded, his jaw clenched tight against the pain radiating through his shoulder. "I know. We need an exit strategy, and fast."

As he scanned their surroundings, Duggins felt the weight of command pressing down on him. The lives of his team, the success of the mission, all hung in the balance. And with each passing second, their chances of survival dwindled.

Duggins' eyes locked onto a narrow alleyway to their left, partially obscured by smoke and debris. "There," he barked, gesturing with his chin. "Jose, pop smoke. We're making a run for it."

Jose nodded, his face etched with exhaustion and determination. He pulled the pin on a smoke grenade and hurled it towards the enemy's position. Within seconds, thick plumes of gray smoke billowed outward, providing a temporary veil.

"Move! Now!" Duggins shouted, hefting Ali-Shabaab's limp form over his shoulder. The wounded man groaned weakly, barely clinging to consciousness.

The team sprang into action, years of training kicking in as they executed a coordinated retreat. Duggins grunted under Ali-Shabaab's weight, each step sending jolts of pain through his injured shoulder. Sweat stung his eyes as he pushed forward, his mind racing. *How far until we're clear? Can Ali-Shabaab hold on that long?*

They weaved through the narrow alleyways, the sounds of pursuit growing fainter behind them. Jose took point, his weapon at the ready, while another team member covered their six.

"Sir," Jose whispered urgently, "I think I see a way out. There's an abandoned warehouse about fifty meters ahead. We could regroup there, assess our situation."

Duggins nodded, his breath coming in ragged gasps. "Good call. Let's move."

As they approached the warehouse, a sudden burst of gunfire erupted from their flank. Bullets ricocheted off nearby walls, showering them with fragments.

"Contact left!" Jose shouted, returning fire.

Duggins' heart pounded as he realized they were mere steps from relative safety. He gritted his teeth, summoning his last reserves of strength. "Cover me!" he yelled, making a final sprint toward the warehouse door.

Just as he reached the threshold, a searing pain tore through his leg. Duggins stumbled, nearly dropping Ali-Shabaab as he crashed through the doorway. He hit the ground hard, the world spinning around him.

As darkness crept into the edges of his vision, Duggins heard the frantic voices of his team. He struggled to focus, to give orders, but his strength was fading fast.

The last thing he saw before losing consciousness was Ali-Shabaab's face, the man's eyes suddenly clear and alert, a ghost of a smile playing across his lips.

CHAPTER 13

The flickering fluorescent light cast long shadows across the faces of the C.O.R.E. team huddled in the cramped safehouse room. Arthur Duggins' weathered features were a mask of tension as he paced the creaking floorboards, each step punctuated by the muffled sounds of distant gunfire.

"We're running out of time," he growled, more to himself than the others. His piercing gaze swept over his exhausted operatives. "Martinez, status report on our exfil route?"

"Three potential choke points, sir," Martinez replied, her voice hoarse. "Local militia activity has increased in the last hour."

Duggins nodded curtly, his mind racing through contingencies. The weight of command pressed down on him like a physical force. Had he made the right call bringing them here? The mission was unraveling, and the blood of innocents in Tel Aviv would be on his hands if they failed.

"Sir?" Cooper's hesitant voice broke through Duggins' spiraling thoughts. "What's our next move?"

Duggins halted his pacing, forcing his features into a mask of calm authority he didn't feel. "We adapt. We survive. We complete the mission." The words felt hollow, even as he said them.

"With all due respect," Ramirez interjected, "how the hell are we supposed to do that when our intel's gone to shit and we're pinned down in this rathole?"

The accusation in Ramirez's tone struck Duggins like a physical blow. *He's right,* a traitorous voice whispered in his mind. *You've led them into a trap.*

"We improvise," Duggins replied, injecting steel into his voice. "That's what we're trained for. Cooper, I need you on comms. See if you can re-establish contact with home base. Martinez, Ramirez – gear check. We move in ten."

As his team sprang into action, Duggins resumed his restless pacing. Each step echoed with doubt. The fate of countless lives hung in the balance, and the crushing weight of responsibility threatened to overwhelm him. He clenched his fists, willing himself to focus on the mission parameters, on the next decisive action that could turn the tide.

But the guilt gnawed at him, insidious and relentless. Had he become too cautious? Too reckless? The line between prudence and paralysis had never seemed so razor-thin.

"Sir?" Cooper's voice cut through the maelstrom of Duggins' thoughts. "I've got something."

Duggins moved to the makeshift comm station, hope warring with dread in his chest. "Talk to me."

Duggins turned away from Cooper, his jaw clenched as he processed the latest update. His eyes fell upon the far corner of the dimly lit room, where a figure lay motionless on a crude pallet.

Ali-Shabaab's chest rose and fell in shallow, labored breaths. His face, etched with lines of pain, glistened with a sheen of sweat. Yet even in his weakened state, his eyes flickered with an intensity that belied his physical condition. Those dark orbs darted around the room, cataloging every detail with predatory focus.

Duggins approached the makeshift bed, each step measured and deliberate. His hand instinctively brushed the grip of his sidearm as he towered over the prone form of their enigmatic informant.

"Alright, Ali," Duggins growled, his voice low and edged with frustration. "Playtime's over. I need answers, and I need them now."

Ali-Shabaab's gaze locked onto Duggins, a hint of defiance flickering beneath the haze of pain. "What... answers do you seek, Captain?" he rasped, his accent thickening each word.

Duggins leaned in close, his face inches from Ali-Shabaab's. "Let's start with why our mission went sideways. Who compromised us? And don't give me any more of your cryptic bullshit. Lives are on the line."

Ali-Shabaab's lips twisted into what might have been a smile or a grimace. "The truth... is rarely simple, Captain. Your enemies... are not always who you think they are."

Duggins fought the urge to grab the man by his shirt collar. Stay cool, he reminded himself. Push too hard, and you might lose what little cooperation he's offering. But time was running out, and with it, his patience.

"I'm not here for riddles," Duggins snapped. "Who's the real target? What are we missing?"

Ali-Shabaab's eyes flickered, a shadow of something—amusement? fear?—passing across his face. "The bomb... is merely a distraction," he whispered, his voice barely audible. "The real threat... lies in the shadows of your own ranks."

Duggins felt his blood run cold. What the hell did that mean? He opened his mouth to demand clarification, but Ali-Shabaab's eyes had already begun to close, his energy seemingly spent.

"Dammit," Duggins muttered, straightening up. He turned to his team, who had been silently observing the exchange. "Pack it up. We're moving out."

The room erupted into controlled chaos as the team sprang into action. Duggins watched as they efficiently gathered their gear, each member moving with practiced precision. Thompson checked his medical supplies, while Rodriguez double-checked the ammunition.

As Duggins retrieved his own pack, his mind raced. Ali-Shabaab's words echoed in his head, a maddening puzzle with potentially devastating consequences. A mole in their ranks? Or was it another layer of deception?

"Sir," Chen's voice cut through his thoughts. "We're ready."

Duggins nodded, shouldering his pack. "Remember, people, time is not on our side. We move fast, we move quiet. Questions?"

Silence met his query, each face set with grim determination.

"Alright," Duggins said, moving towards the door. "Let's go save Tel Aviv."

Duggins pressed his ear against the compound's heavy metal door, his breath shallow as he strained to hear any signs of movement outside. The team huddled behind him, weapons at the ready, their bodies taut with tension.

"On my mark," Duggins whispered, his hand raised. He met each team member's eyes, seeing his own mix of fear and determination reflected back. With a silent nod, he slowly pushed the door open.

The night air hit them like a wall, thick with the acrid smell of smoke and gunpowder. Duggins scanned the immediate area, his eyes adjusting to the dim streetlights. Debris littered the ground, remnants of recent battles.

"Clear," he breathed, motioning the team forward.

As they emerged from the compound, Virginia Turner fell in step beside Duggins. "Arthur," she murmured, her voice low and urgent, "what exactly did Ali-Shabaab mean about the shadows in our ranks?"

Duggins clenched his jaw, torn between the need for secrecy and the potential threat to his team. "Not now, Virginia," he hissed. "Stay focused on getting us out of here alive."

They moved swiftly through the war-torn streets, their footsteps muffled by the distant sounds of gunfire and explosions. The chaos of Baghdad surrounded them, a symphony of destruction that both concealed their movements and threatened to engulf them.

Jose Beals took point, his muscular frame tense as he navigated through the rubble. Suddenly, he raised a fist, signaling the team to halt. In the distance, the unmistakable sound of an approaching patrol reached their ears.

"Shit," Duggins thought, his mind racing through their options. "Alleyway, three o'clock," he whispered, gesturing to a narrow passage between two bombed-out buildings.

As they pressed themselves against the crumbling walls, Duggins caught a glimpse of Ali-Shabaab's face. Despite his injuries, the man's eyes were alert, taking in every detail of their surroundings. What game was he playing?

The patrol passed by, their voices carried on the wind. Duggins held his breath, acutely aware of how exposed they were. One wrong move, one misplaced step, and their mission—and their lives—would be over.

As the voices faded, Duggins exhaled slowly, his keen eyes scanning the alley's exit. "We're clear. Move out, stay low."

The team slipped back into the labyrinth of backstreets, Duggins leading them through a complex series of turns. His mind raced, recalling every detail from countless missions and intel briefings.

"Sir," whispered Kowalski, her voice tight with tension, "shouldn't we be heading east?"

Duggins shook his head, responding in clipped tones. "Negative. Enemy's expecting that. We're looping around, using the old market as cover."

They pressed on, the weight of their gear and the injured Ali-Shabaab slowing their pace. Duggins' instincts screamed danger at every corner, but he pushed the fear down, focusing on the path ahead.

Suddenly, the unmistakable click of a weapon being readied echoed from a nearby doorway. Duggins reacted instantly, shoving Virginia and Ali-Shabaab behind a pile of rubble as a spray of bullets tore through the air where they'd been standing.

"Contact front!" Beals shouted, returning fire.

Duggins' heart pounded, adrenaline surging through his veins. He caught Ali-Shabaab's eye, noting the man's eerily calm demeanor. "You knew this would happen," Duggins growled, suspicion flaring. "Who else knows we're here?"

Before Ali-Shabaab could answer, another burst of gunfire erupted, forcing Duggins back into the fight. He pushed the questions aside, knowing survival came first. But the seed of doubt had been planted, and it would not be easily uprooted.

The team burst through a rusted metal door, stumbling into the cavernous interior of an abandoned warehouse. Duggins scanned the area, his trained eyes picking out potential threats and escape routes.

"Secure the perimeter," he ordered, his voice barely above a whisper. "Kowalski, tend to Ali-Shabaab."

As the team spread out, Duggins pressed his back against a crumbling concrete wall, his chest heaving. The coolness of the surface seeped through his sweat-soaked shirt, a stark contrast to the oppressive heat outside. He closed his eyes for a moment, allowing himself a brief respite.

"Clear," came the hushed reports from his team.

Duggins nodded, gathering them close. Their faces were etched with exhaustion and tension, mirroring his own internal struggle. He took a deep breath, steadying himself.

"Listen up," he began, his voice low but firm. "We're not out of the woods yet. That ambush wasn't random. Someone's onto us, and we need to stay three steps ahead."

Virginia's eyes narrowed. "You think we've got a mole?"

Duggins held her gaze. "I think we can't rule anything out. From here on, we trust no one but each other. Understood?"

A chorus of nods answered him.

"Good. Now, here's the plan..."

As Duggins outlined their next moves, he couldn't shake the nagging feeling that they were missing something crucial. Ali-Shabaab's cryptic words echoed in his mind, a puzzle he couldn't quite solve. But there was no time for doubt. The lives of his team – and countless others – depended on his leadership.

"Remember," he concluded, his voice filled with quiet determination, "we're the only thing standing between these terrorists and their target. Stay focused, stay alert, and above all, stay together. We finish this mission, or we die trying."

The weight of his words hung in the air, a solemn pact among warriors. Duggins met each of their eyes in turn, drawing strength from their unwavering resolve. Whatever came next, they would face it as one.

Duggins turned to the makeshift intelligence center they'd assembled in the corner of the abandoned building. Laptops hummed softly, their screens casting an eerie glow on the team's faces as they huddled around.

"Alright, what have we got?" Duggins asked, his voice tense.

Virginia's fingers flew across her keyboard. "I've cross-referenced Ali-Shabaab's ramblings with our existing intel. There's a pattern emerging, but it's... elusive."

Duggins leaned in, his brow furrowed. "Show me."

A map of Tel Aviv flickered to life on the screen, dotted with potential targets. As Virginia explained her findings, Duggins felt the pieces start to click into place.

"Wait," he interrupted, pointing to a seemingly innocuous location. "That warehouse. Ali-Shabaab mentioned 'the heart of the beast.' What if he didn't mean it metaphorically?"

The team exchanged glances, realization dawning.

"It's central, unassuming, and..." Thompson's voice trailed off as he pulled up blueprints. "Jesus. It's right above the city's main power grid."

Duggins felt a chill run down his spine. "That's it. They're not just planning an attack; they're going to plunge the entire city into chaos."

As the implications sank in, Duggins' mind raced. They had the target, but time was running out. He made a split-second decision.

"Gear up. We move in five."

The team sprang into action, their movements precise and practiced. As Duggins checked his weapon, he caught a glimpse of Ali-Shabaab's haunted eyes in his memory. What else was the enigmatic informant hiding?

No time to dwell on it now. They had a city to save.

Minutes later, they emerged from the building, moving swiftly through the shadows. Duggins took point, every sense on high alert. As they navigated the war-torn streets, the weight of their mission pressed down on him.

"Stay sharp," he murmured into his comm. "We're walking into the lion's den."

With each step, their resolve hardened. They were the last line of defense, and failure was not an option. As they approached their target, Duggins steeled himself for the fight ahead. Whatever came next, they were ready.

THE EXTRACTION

As they rounded the final corner, the nondescript building loomed before them, its mundane exterior belying the potential devastation housed within. Duggins felt a surge of adrenaline, his heart pounding in his ears.

"Remember," he whispered, his voice barely audible, "we're ghosts. In and out, no traces."

Jose nodded, his eyes scanning the perimeter. "Two guards, north entrance. Another on the roof."

Raven materialized beside them, her voice a low murmur. "I can take care of the rooftop sentry. Give me two minutes."

Duggins hesitated, studying Raven's impassive face. Could he trust her? He had no choice.

"Go," he ordered, then turned to the others. "We breach on my signal."

As Raven melted into the shadows, Duggins' mind raced. What if this was all part of a larger trap? What if Ali-Shabaab's cryptic warnings were leading them straight into danger?

He pushed the doubts aside, focusing on the mission. Tel Aviv's fate hung in the balance, and they were the only ones who could tip the scales.

"Now," he breathed into his comm, and they surged forward, silent as wraiths.

As they crossed the threshold into unknown territory, Duggins couldn't shake the feeling that they were stepping into something far bigger than they'd anticipated. Whatever lay ahead, there was no turning back now.

CHAPTER 14

The stench of sweat and gunpowder hung heavy in the air as Arthur Duggins surveyed the dimly lit room. His team huddled around a makeshift bed, their faces etched with tension. On the bed lay Ali Shabaab, his chest rising and falling in shallow, labored breaths. The informant's eyes flickered with an urgent intensity that sent a chill down Duggins' spine.

Duggins leaned in, his imposing frame casting a shadow over the dying man. "Ali, we need that information now. Lives are at stake." His voice was firm, laced with the authority of years in the field.

Ali's eyes locked onto Duggins', a hint of defiance flashing beneath the pain. "Patience... is a virtue... even in war," he rasped, each word a struggle.

Duggins clenched his jaw, fighting the urge to shake the man. *We don't have time for games.* He took a deep breath, forcing his voice to remain steady. "Look, I know you're in pain, but every second counts. Tell us what you know about the attack."

Ali's lips curled into a ghost of a smile. "The answer... lies in the whispers... of the ancient city."

Cryptic bastard. Duggins' mind raced, trying to decipher the meaning behind the words. He glanced at his team, their faces a mix of frustration and determination.

"Ali, please," Duggins implored, leaning closer. "We can't save lives with riddles. Give us something concrete."

The informant's breathing grew more labored, his eyes losing focus. Duggins felt a surge of panic. We're losing him.

"Time... is not linear," Ali mumbled, his voice barely above a whisper. "The past... holds the key... to the future."

Duggins fought back a growl of frustration. "Damn it, Ali! People will die if we don't stop this attack. Is that what you want?"

For a moment, clarity seemed to return to Ali's eyes. He reached out, grasping Duggins' arm with surprising strength. "The answer... is in plain sight... if you know... where to look."

As Ali's hand fell away, Duggins straightened up, his mind whirling. What the hell does that mean? He looked at his team, seeing his own confusion mirrored in their faces. Time was running out, and they were no closer to stopping the impending disaster.

THE EXTRACTION

Duggins ran a hand through his hair, his mind racing. "Alright team, let's break this down. Ancient city, non-linear time, past and future, hiding in plain sight. What are we missing?"

Sarah, his tech expert, piped up. "Could 'ancient city' refer to Jerusalem? It's got layers of history, fits the bill."

"Possible," Duggins nodded, his eyes never leaving Ali's face. The informant's breathing was growing more ragged by the second.

Ali's eyes flickered open, his gaze intense despite his weakening state. "The clock... strikes thirteen... when the sun... kisses the dome."

Duggins leaned in, hanging on every word. "Clock strikes thirteen? That's impossible unless..."

"Unless it's not a regular clock," Jake, the demolitions expert, interjected. "Could be a code, or a specific location."

Ali's hand shot out, gripping Duggins' wrist. "The golden... hour... reveals all."

Duggins' mind raced, piecing together the fragments. "Golden hour... sunset? And a dome... The Dome of the Rock?"

The team huddled closer, the tension palpable. Duggins could almost hear the gears turning in their heads as they grappled with Ali's cryptic clues.

"Boss," Sarah whispered, her eyes wide. "What if the 'clock' is the shadow cast by the Dome at sunset? Thirteen could be a specific angle or position."

Duggins nodded, feeling they were on the verge of a breakthrough. But time was running out, for both them and Ali. He turned back to the informant, desperate for more information, only to find Ali's eyes closed, his breathing shallow.

"Stay with us, Ali," Duggins urged, his voice a mix of command and plea. "We need more. Where exactly is the attack going to happen?"

Duggins' mind raced, synapses firing as he pieced together the fragmented clues. The Dome of the Rock, sunset, a shadow forming an impossible "13" - it was all starting to coalesce into a coherent picture.

"The bombs," he muttered, more to himself than the team. "They're using the shadow as a timer. When it hits that specific angle..."

Sarah leaned in, her brow furrowed. "But where exactly, boss? The Old City's a maze."

Duggins' eyes narrowed, recalling a detail from their intel briefing. "The Western Wall plaza. It's the only place with a clear view of the Dome that could accommodate multiple devices."

Jake nodded grimly. "Makes sense. Maximum casualties, maximum symbolic impact."

Duggins straightened, his mind already formulating a plan. "We'll need to split into two teams. One to evacuate, one to locate and disarm. We'll need local support, gear from-"

A deafening roar cut him off mid-sentence. The world exploded into chaos as the safehouse walls buckled inward. Duggins' training kicked in instantly, his body moving before his mind could process. He dove for cover, feeling the sting of debris pelting his back.

"Contact!" he shouted over the ringing in his ears. "Everyone, sta-"

Another explosion rocked the building, closer this time. Duggins' heart raced, adrenaline surging. They'd been compromised, but how? His eyes darted to Ali, still motionless on the makeshift bed. Had they been betrayed, or simply found?

No time to dwell on it now. They needed to move, to secure their intel and get out alive. Duggins opened his mouth to bark orders, praying his team had survived the initial blast.

The air filled with dust and the acrid smell of explosives as Duggins' team sprang into action. Jake dove behind an overturned table, his rifle already at the ready. Sarah crawled towards the shattered window, seeking a vantage point.

"Status!" Duggins barked, his voice cutting through the chaos.

"Clear left!" Jake shouted.

"Right side compromised!" Sarah reported, her voice tense. "Multiple hostiles approaching!"

Duggins' mind raced, assessing their options. The safehouse had become a deathtrap, but they couldn't leave without Ali-Shabaab and the critical information he held.

"Sarah, cover fire! Jake, secure our exit!" Duggins ordered, his tone brooking no argument.

THE EXTRACTION

As gunfire erupted outside, Duggins locked eyes with Ali-Shabaab. The informant's face was a mask of pain and determination. Without hesitation, Duggins lunged towards him.

"I've got you," Duggins grunted, wrapping his arms around Ali-Shabaab's frail form. He could feel the man's labored breathing against his chest.

A bullet whizzed past Duggins' ear as he maneuvered Ali-Shabaab behind a fallen support beam. Debris rained down around them, but Duggins shielded the dying man with his own body.

"Stay with me," Duggins urged, his voice low and intense. "We're not done yet."

Ali-Shabaab's eyes flickered open, a ghost of a smile on his lips. "You... are a man of honor, Duggins," he wheezed.

Duggins felt a pang of guilt. Honor had little place in their world of shadows and half-truths. But right now, all that mattered was keeping Ali-Shabaab alive long enough to finish what they'd started.

Duggins scanned the room, his piercing eyes cutting through the settling dust. "Regroup!" he commanded, his voice a steady anchor amidst the chaos. The team converged around him, their faces etched with determination despite the fresh cuts and bruises.

"We're not out of this yet," Duggins stated, his tone brooking no argument. "Our mission remains unchanged. Ali-Shabaab, we need those remaining clues. Lives are at stake."

Ali-Shabaab's eyes flickered open, his gaze locking onto Duggins with an intensity that belied his weakened state. "The desert... holds secrets," he whispered, his voice barely audible over the distant sounds of conflict. "Where the sun... kisses the dunes... at dawn."

Duggins' mind raced, parsing the cryptic words. Desert. Sunrise. But where? He needed more.

"Keep going," Duggins urged, leaning closer. "What else can you tell us?"

Ali-Shabaab's breathing grew more labored, each word a struggle. "The falcon's... nest... high above... the city of gold."

Sarah interjected, her voice tense. "Falcon's nest? Could be a reference to a high-rise building."

THE EXTRACTION

Duggins nodded, his brain working overtime to piece together the puzzle. "City of gold... Dubai, maybe? But that doesn't fit with the desert clue."

Ali-Shabaab's hand suddenly gripped Duggins' arm with surprising strength. "Time... is short," he gasped. "The key... lies in the... ancient text."

As the dying man's words faded, Duggins felt the weight of responsibility pressing down on him. They had the clues, but deciphering them in time seemed an almost insurmountable task. Yet, he knew failure wasn't an option.

"Alright, team," Duggins said, his voice firm and resolute. "We've got work to do. Every second counts."

Duggins stood abruptly, his mind racing as he paced the small room. The team watched him intently, recognizing the telltale signs of their leader on the verge of a breakthrough.

"Desert, sunrise, falcon's nest, city of gold, ancient text," Duggins muttered, his piercing eyes narrowed in concentration. Suddenly, he snapped his fingers. "It's not Dubai. It's Tel Aviv."

Sarah raised an eyebrow. "How'd you figure that, boss?"

Duggins turned to face his team, his expression grim but determined. "The 'White City' - Tel Aviv's nickname. It's often called the 'city of gold' because of how the sunlight reflects off the Bauhaus architecture at dawn."

He continued, his words coming faster now. "The falcon's nest - it's got to be a high point overlooking the city. And the ancient text..." Duggins paused, his eyes widening. "The Dead Sea Scrolls. They're housed in the Shrine of the Book, which looks like a white dome rising from the ground."

"So where's the bomb?" asked Mike, leaning forward intently.

Duggins' jaw clenched. "My bet? The Israel Museum. It fits all the clues and would be a devastating target."

The team exchanged worried glances as Duggins began formulating a plan. "We're running out of time. Sarah, contact our asset in Tel Aviv PD. We'll need a clear route to the museum. Mike, get on the horn with local counterterrorism. We'll need backup, but keep it quiet. Last thing we need is widespread panic."

As his team sprang into action, Duggins found himself staring at the wall, his mind already racing ahead to the challenges they'd face.

The streets of Tel Aviv would be a war zone, and they were working against the clock.

"We've got one shot at this," he thought, a mixture of determination and anxiety churning in his gut. "Failure isn't an option. Not with so many lives at stake."

The safehouse erupted into a flurry of activity. Duggins' team moved with practiced efficiency, their actions betraying the urgency of the situation. The clatter of equipment and hushed voices filled the air as they gathered their gear.

Duggins surveyed the room, his piercing eyes taking in every detail. "Listen up," he called out, his voice cutting through the noise. The team immediately fell silent, all eyes turning to their leader.

"We're operating on borrowed time," Duggins continued, his tone steady but laced with intensity. "Sarah, you're on point. I need you to clear our route to the museum. Use every contact you've got."

Sarah nodded sharply, already reaching for her comm device.

"Mike, you're our eyes in the sky. I want real-time satellite imagery of the area surrounding the museum. Look for anything out of place, no matter how small."

Mike's fingers flew over his tablet, pulling up the necessary systems.

Duggins turned to the rest of the team. "Johnson, you're on demolitions. Be ready for anything. Torres, you're our infiltration specialist. I need you thinking three steps ahead of any security measures we might encounter."

As he spoke, Duggins felt the familiar tightening in his chest - the weight of command, of lives hanging in the balance. He pushed it aside, focusing on the task at hand.

"Remember," he said, his voice dropping to a near growl, "we're the only thing standing between Tel Aviv and catastrophe. Whatever it takes, we disarm that bomb. Questions?"

The team's silence spoke volumes. They were ready.

Duggins nodded, a grim smile touching his lips. "Then let's move out. We've got a city to save."

As Duggins pushed open the safehouse door, the world erupted into chaos. A hail of bullets tore through the air, shattering the night's silence and sending splinters of wood flying.

"Contact!" Duggins roared, diving for cover behind an overturned dumpster. His heart pounded, adrenaline surging through his veins. "Multiple hostiles, nine o'clock!"

Jose's voice crackled over the comm. "I've got eyes on three shooters, rooftop across the street!"

Duggins' mind raced, assessing their options. The mission, the bomb, the countless lives at stake – all hung by a thread. He couldn't let it end here, not when they were so close.

"Sarah, suppressing fire!" he ordered, his voice cutting through the cacophony of gunshots. "Mike, find us an exit route!"

As Sarah's rifle barked in response, Duggins risked a glance around the dumpster. The muzzle flashes from the rooftop illuminated shadowy figures, their intentions as clear as the danger they posed.

"Jose, on me!" Duggins called out. "We're going to flank left, try to outmaneuver them."

As they moved, keeping low and using the scattered debris for cover, Duggins felt a familiar pang of worry for his team. He pushed it aside, focusing on the task at hand.

"Sir," Mike's voice came through, tight with tension. "I've got a possible route, but it's risky. Narrow alley, fifty meters to your three o'clock."

Duggins weighed the options, knowing each second could mean the difference between success and catastrophic failure. "Copy that. Team, prepare to move on my mark. We're going to make a run for it."

He took a deep breath, steadying himself. The weight of command had never felt heavier. "Remember," he said, his voice low and intense, "we're the only ones who can stop this attack. Whatever happens, the mission comes first. Understood?"

A chorus of affirmatives echoed through the comm.

Duggins nodded, steeling himself. "On three. One... two..."

CHAPTER 15

The fluorescent lights flickered in the underground bunker as Arthur Duggins surveyed his team. Their faces, etched with determination, looked back at him expectantly. He felt the weight of their trust, the burden of command settling on his shoulders like a familiar cloak.

"Listen up," Duggins said, his voice cutting through the tense silence. "We've got Ali-Shabaab's final clues. The bastard's playing games, but we don't have time for that luxury."

He tapped a button, and a holographic map of Tel Aviv sprang to life in the center of the room. Red markers pulsed ominously at various points across the city.

"These are our potential targets," Duggins continued, his finger tracing a path between the markers. "Ali-Shabaab's intel suggests multiple strike points, designed to maximize chaos and casualties."

As he spoke, Duggins couldn't help but recall Ali-Shabaab's measured voice, the careful cadence that revealed just enough to be tantalizing, but never enough to give them a clear advantage. The memory sent a chill down his spine.

"Sir," Agent Reeves interjected, her brow furrowed. "How reliable is this information? Ali-Shabaab's not exactly known for his honesty."

Duggins nodded, acknowledging the valid concern. "Trust me, I've considered that. But my gut tells me this is legit. The stakes are too high to ignore it."

He zoomed in on a particular section of the map, highlighting a bustling commercial district. "This area here is our primary focus. High foot traffic, multiple entry points, perfect for their MO."

As he detailed the potential attack scenarios, Duggins felt a familiar surge of adrenaline. The thrill of the hunt, tempered by the grave responsibility of preventing mass casualties. He pushed aside thoughts of past missions, of close calls and narrow escapes. This was here and now, and failure wasn't an option.

"We're on a tight timeline, people," Duggins said, his voice carrying the weight of urgency. "Every second counts. We move out in thirty minutes. Gear up, check your comms, and be ready for anything."

As his team dispersed to prepare, Duggins found himself staring at the holographic map, the red markers seeming to pulse in time with his heartbeat. He couldn't shake the feeling that Ali-Shabaab was watching, waiting, always one step ahead.

"Not this time," Duggins muttered to himself, his jaw set with determination. "This time, we end it."

Duggins tore his gaze from the map, turning to face his team. "Alright, let's dig deeper. I want everyone's insights on this. No idea is too outlandish, no connection too tenuous. Speak up."

Sarah, their tech specialist, stepped forward. "The timing of these messages is odd. They all came in at exactly 17 minutes past the hour, regardless of which hour. Could be a code?"

Duggins nodded, his mind racing. "Good catch. What else?"

Jake, the weapons expert, chimed in. "The references to 'birds of prey' keep popping up. Might be literal - drones, maybe?"

As the team bounced ideas back and forth, Duggins felt a familiar tension in his shoulders. He'd seen this dance before - the frantic search for meaning in a sea of cryptic clues. But something about Ali-Shabaab's intel felt different. More... personal.

"What if we're looking at this all wrong?" Duggins interrupted, his voice cutting through the chatter. "Ali-Shabaab isn't just giving us information. He's challenging us."

He pulled up one of the messages on the main screen. "Look at this phrase: 'The answer lies where the sun touches the sea.' It's not just a clue, it's a taunt."

Duggins' mind raced, piecing together fragments of intel. "He's playing a game with us, testing our skills. Each clue is a piece of a larger puzzle."

As the team pored over the messages with renewed vigor, Duggins couldn't shake a nagging doubt. Was he leading them down the right path, or straight into a trap? The weight of command pressed down on him, a familiar burden he'd carried for years.

"Time's ticking," he reminded them, pushing aside his doubts. "Let's crack this puzzle before it's too late."

Duggins' eyes darted across the illuminated map of Tel Aviv, his mind racing as he connected the cryptic clues to potential targets. "Here," he said, tapping a location near the coastline. "The Jaffa Port. It fits the 'where the sun touches the sea' reference."

He moved his finger to another spot. "The Azrieli Center towers. Tallest buildings in the city - perfect for 'birds of prey.'"

THE EXTRACTION

As Duggins marked each location, the gravity of the situation settled over the room. He could feel the tension radiating from his team, a mix of anticipation and dread.

"We've got five potential targets," Duggins announced, his voice steady despite the churning in his gut. "We need to split up and investigate each one."

He turned to face his team, studying their determined faces. These were the best of the best, but even they couldn't hide the flicker of apprehension in their eyes.

"Johnson, you take the port. Rivera, the Azrieli Center. Chang, cover the Carmel Market." Duggins assigned the remaining locations, his mind already formulating contingency plans.

As the team gathered their gear, Duggins pulled aside his second-in-command. "Watch your backs out there," he muttered, his voice low. "This feels... different. Ali-Shabaab's playing for keeps this time."

The operative nodded, understanding the unspoken concern in Duggins' words. As the teams filed out, Duggins couldn't shake the feeling that they were walking into something far more complex than they realized. But there was no time for doubt. The clock was ticking, and Tel Aviv's fate hung in the balance.

Duggins settled into the makeshift command center, his eyes flicking between multiple screens displaying real-time feeds from his team's body cameras. The hum of equipment filled the air as he adjusted his headset, his voice calm but authoritative.

"Team leaders, check in. Status reports every fifteen minutes or immediately if you encounter anything suspicious."

As acknowledgments crackled through the comm system, Duggins leaned forward, scanning the feeds intently. His weathered fingers tapped a rapid rhythm on the desk, betraying the tension coiled within him.

"Rivera, movement on your six," he warned, spotting a figure lurking in the shadows near the Azrieli Center. "Could be nothing, but stay alert."

Rivera's voice came back, terse but controlled. "Copy that. Proceeding with caution."

Duggins' mind raced, analyzing every detail. Something about this operation felt off, like trying to complete a puzzle with missing pieces. He pushed the unease aside, focusing on the task at hand.

THE EXTRACTION

Suddenly, Chang's voice cut through, urgent and breathless. "Duggins, we've got company at the Carmel Market. Two men, heavily armed. Definitely not local security."

Duggins' jaw clenched. "Engage only if necessary. Try to gather intel without being detected."

As he coordinated Chang's team through the market's labyrinthine alleys, Johnson's feed from the port erupted into chaos. Gunfire echoed through the comm system, and Duggins watched helplessly as Johnson's camera jerked wildly.

"Johnson, report!" Duggins barked, his calm exterior cracking.

"Ambush!" Johnson's reply came between ragged breaths. "These aren't Ali-Shabaab. Different tactics, different gear. I think we've stumbled into—"

The transmission cut off abruptly, leaving Duggins staring at static. His mind raced through possibilities, each more alarming than the last. Had they underestimated the situation? Were there more players in this game than they realized?

"All teams, fall back to secondary rendezvous points," Duggins ordered, his voice steady despite the turmoil in his gut. "We may have stirred up a hornet's nest here. Watch your backs and trust no one."

As he watched his teams navigate the treacherous streets of Tel Aviv, Duggins couldn't shake the feeling that they'd just scratched the surface of something far more sinister than they'd anticipated. The rival groups weren't just surveilling them; they were actively engaging. But why? What were they protecting, or perhaps, what were they after?

Duggins leaned back, his mind churning with possibilities and strategies. One thing was clear: the stakes had just been raised, and the true nature of their mission was only beginning to reveal itself.

Duggins' fingers flew across the keyboard, pulling up satellite imagery of Tel Aviv. His eyes darted between the screen and the comm panel, where intermittent bursts of static mixed with hurried reports from his scattered teams.

"Martinez, what's your status?" he demanded, his voice taut with tension.

"We've cleared the market district," Martinez replied, her words punctuated by heavy breaths. "But we've got shadows. Two men, possibly armed. They're good, sir. Real good."

Duggins' jaw clenched. "Keep moving. Change your route every three blocks. I'm sending you a new path now."

As he uploaded the alternative route, Duggins' mind raced. These weren't standard terrorist tactics. The level of coordination, the sophistication of their opponents - it all pointed to something bigger.

"Sir," Chen's voice crackled through the comm, "we've found something at the docks. It's... it's not what we expected."

"Talk to me, Chen," Duggins urged, leaning forward.

"It's a shipment manifest. But the cargo... it's not weapons. It's tech. Advanced tech. The kind you'd use for a massive cyber attack."

Duggins felt a chill run down his spine. A cyber attack? That hadn't been part of any intel they'd received. His mind whirled with the implications.

"All teams," he announced, his voice carrying a newfound urgency, "converge on extraction point Delta. We need to regroup and reassess."

As his operatives acknowledged the order, Duggins stood, pacing the small command center. They'd been so focused on a physical attack, they'd missed the signs of a digital threat. But why Tel Aviv? What was the true target?

The pieces were there, he knew. They just needed to put them together.

Arthur Duggins stood at the head of the table, his weathered hands splayed across a map of Tel Aviv. His piercing eyes scanned the faces of his team, each member tense with anticipation.

"Alright, people," he began, his voice low and measured. "We've got a new ballgame. The physical attack was a smokescreen. Their real target is digital."

He tapped a series of locations on the map. "These are the primary data centers in Tel Aviv. Based on the tech manifest Chen found, they're likely aiming to cripple Israel's cyber infrastructure."

Duggins' mind raced, considering angles and contingencies. "We'll split into three teams. Alpha will secure the main data center here," he pointed, "while Bravo and Charlie create a perimeter and hunt down any hostiles in the vicinity."

THE EXTRACTION

As he spoke, Duggins felt the familiar weight of responsibility settle on his shoulders. Every decision could mean life or death, not just for his team, but for countless civilians.

"Questions?" he asked, his gaze sweeping the room.

Chen raised her hand. "Sir, what if we're wrong? What if there's still a physical component to the attack?"

Duggins nodded, appreciating her foresight. "Good point, Chen. That's why Delta team will remain mobile, ready to respond to any unexpected threats."

He took a deep breath, steeling himself for what was to come. "Gear up, people. We move in thirty."

The room burst into activity. Duggins moved to the weapons locker, methodically checking each piece of equipment. As he loaded his sidearm, a flicker of doubt crossed his mind. Had he considered every angle? Was he leading his team into a trap?

He pushed the thoughts aside. Doubt was a luxury he couldn't afford right now. His team was counting on him, and he wouldn't let them down.

Arthur Duggins stood before his team, their faces a mix of determination and tension. The weight of the mission pressed down on him, but he drew strength from their unwavering trust. He cleared his throat, his voice low and steady.

"Listen up, people. We've trained for this. We've bled for this. Every mission, every sleepless night, every sacrifice has led us to this moment." Duggins' eyes locked with each team member in turn. "The stakes couldn't be higher. Thousands of innocent lives hang in the balance."

He paced, his movements deliberate. "But I've seen what this team can do. We're not just soldiers; we're the last line of defense against chaos. Remember, we're not fighting for some abstract concept. We're fighting for every child who deserves to grow up without fear, for every family that deserves peace."

Duggins' voice grew fiercer. "When we land in Tel Aviv, we hit the ground running. Trust your instincts, trust your training, and above all, trust each other. We go in as a team, and we come out as a team. No one gets left behind."

He paused, his gaze intense. "Any questions?"

THE EXTRACTION

Silence filled the room. Duggins nodded, a grim smile on his face. "Then let's move out."

As they boarded the plane, Duggins felt the familiar surge of adrenaline. His mind raced through scenarios, contingencies, potential pitfalls. He glanced at his team, their faces set with determination.

Chen caught his eye. "We've got this, sir," she said quietly.

Duggins nodded, grateful for her confidence. As the engines roared to life, he closed his eyes briefly. The weight of command pressed down on him, but he welcomed it. This was what he was made for.

The plane lifted off, carrying them towards Tel Aviv and the impending threat. Duggins' heart pounded, a mix of anticipation and apprehension coursing through his veins. Whatever challenges lay ahead, he knew one thing for certain: his team was ready.

The wheels of the C-130 screeched against the tarmac as Tel Aviv's Ben Gurion Airport materialized beneath them. Duggins' eyes snapped open, his body instantly alert. Through the small window, he caught glimpses of the sprawling cityscape, its modern skyline a stark contrast to the ancient land it inhabited.

"Gear up," he barked, his voice cutting through the din of the engines. The team moved with practiced efficiency, strapping on body armor and checking weapons.

As they disembarked, the oppressive heat hit Duggins like a physical force. He squinted against the harsh sunlight, scanning the horizon.

"Chen, sitrep," he demanded, his eyes never leaving the perimeter.

"Local assets confirm increased chatter," Chen reported, her voice tight. "Multiple potential targets identified. We're looking at a 6-hour window, max."

Duggins nodded grimly. "Rodriguez, secure transport. Jackson, establish comms with HQ. The rest of you, final equipment check. We move in five."

As his team dispersed, Duggins felt a prickle at the back of his neck. He'd learned to trust that feeling over the years. Something was off.

"Sir," Chen's voice was low, urgent. "We've got company. Three o'clock, black SUV."

Duggins' hand instinctively moved to his sidearm. "Mossad?"

THE EXTRACTION

"Negative. Body language suggests hostiles. Possible rival group."

Duggins' mind raced. How had they been made so quickly? Had Ali-Shabaab's intel been compromised?

"Change of plans," he growled. "We're splitting up. Chen, you're with me. The rest of you, proceed to the primary rendezvous. Go dark until you hear from me."

As his team melted away into the bustling airport, Duggins locked eyes with Chen. "Ready to dance?"

She nodded, a fierce grin on her face. "Always, sir."

Together, they strode towards the waiting SUV, the air crackling with tension. Tel Aviv sprawled before them, a city on the brink. The real battle was about to begin.

CHAPTER 16

The roar of jet engines faded as Arthur Duggins stepped onto the tarmac, immediately assaulted by Tel Aviv's sweltering heat. Sweat beaded on his forehead as he scanned the bustling airport, his hand instinctively reaching for the concealed weapon at his hip.

"Eyes sharp, team," Arthur muttered into his comms. "We're in hostile territory now."

Jose's gruff voice crackled in response, "Roger that, boss. I've got eyes on potential hostiles at our two o'clock."

Arthur's gaze snapped to a group of men eyeing them suspiciously. His muscles tensed, ready for action.

Ali Shabaab materialized beside him, his voice low and calm. "Those men are not a threat. Local security, nothing more."

Arthur's jaw clenched. Ali's presence set him on edge, but he couldn't deny the man's intel had been solid so far. Still, something about him didn't sit right.

As they pushed through the crowded terminal, Arthur's mind raced. How many innocents would die if they failed? The weight of responsibility pressed down on him like a physical force.

Suddenly, Jose's voice cut through his thoughts. "Arthur, we've got incoming intel. Coordinates for multiple bomb sites across the city."

Arthur's pulse quickened. "Understood. Let's move."

They emerged onto Tel Aviv's sun-baked streets, a cacophony of honking horns and shouting voices assaulting their senses. Arthur's eyes darted from face to face, searching for threats.

"First target is two kilometers north," Jose reported. "Heavy civilian presence in the area."

"Damn," Arthur muttered. He turned to his team, noting the determination in their eyes. "Alright, people. We've got a job to do. Lives are at stake. Let's not let them down."

As they moved through the crowded streets, Arthur couldn't shake the feeling that they were being watched. His instincts screamed danger, but there was no time for hesitation. The clock was ticking, and they had a city to save.

Arthur's eyes swept over his team, their faces etched with determination. "We're splitting up. Jose, take Maria and cover the eastern quadrant. Chen, you're with me on the western front. Ali, you're our eyes in the sky. Keep us informed of any suspicious movement."

As the team dispersed, Arthur and Chen moved swiftly through the bustling streets, their senses on high alert. The cacophony of city life masked potential threats, every car a potential bomb, every passerby a possible enemy.

"Chen, what's your read?" Arthur murmured, his hand hovering near his concealed weapon.

Chen's eyes narrowed, scanning the crowd. "Something's off. The air feels... charged."

They rounded a corner, and Arthur's instincts screamed danger. A nondescript van was parked haphazardly, three men in casual clothes loitering nearby. Their stance betrayed military training.

"Contact," Arthur whispered. "Possible hostiles at two o'clock."

Before Chen could respond, one of the men locked eyes with Arthur. Time seemed to freeze for a heartbeat before all hell broke loose.

The air erupted with gunfire. Arthur dove behind a parked car, the ping of bullets striking metal ringing in his ears. "Chen, flank left!" he shouted, returning fire.

The terrorist cell moved with practiced precision, but Arthur and Chen were no amateurs. They weaved through the panicking crowd, using the chaos to their advantage.

A bullet grazed Arthur's arm, and he hissed in pain. "These guys are good," he thought, popping up to squeeze off two more shots. One of the terrorists went down, clutching his leg.

Chen's voice crackled over the comm. "Arthur, I've got eyes on the van. It's rigged!"

Arthur's heart raced. They needed to end this fast. "Cover me!" he yelled, sprinting towards the nearest terrorist. The man's eyes widened in surprise as Arthur closed the distance, his fist connecting with a satisfying crunch.

As they grappled, Arthur couldn't help but marvel at the terrorist's skill. These weren't just fanatics; they were highly trained operatives. The thought chilled him to the bone.

With a final, desperate move, Arthur managed to disarm his opponent. He spun around, weapon raised, to find Chen had neutralized the last terrorist.

Panting heavily, Arthur surveyed the scene. "We need to secure that bomb, now."

As they approached the van, Arthur couldn't shake the feeling that this was just the beginning. What other surprises did these shadowy groups have in store for them?

Across town, Jenna and Marcus weaved through the bustling streets of Tel Aviv, their eyes scanning the crowd for any sign of suspicious activity. The oppressive heat and the crush of bodies made their progress slow and arduous.

"Eyes sharp," Jenna murmured, her hand hovering near her concealed weapon. "These guys could be anyone."

Marcus nodded, his gaze flicking from face to face. "I've got movement on our six. Don't look back."

Jenna's heart rate spiked, but she kept her cool. "Roger that. Let's split up at the next intersection. I'll take point."

As they parted ways, Jenna's earpiece crackled to life. Arthur's voice came through, tight with tension. "Team, we've neutralized a cell at the first location. Be advised, these aren't your average terrorists. They're highly trained and well-equipped."

Jenna ducked into a narrow alley, her mind racing. "Copy that, Arthur. Any intel on the other bomb locations?"

"Negative," Chen's voice replied. "But we're picking up chatter about a possible drop point near the marketplace."

Marcus chimed in, his breath heavy. "I've got two tangos on my tail. Moving to shake them now."

Jenna peered around the corner, spotting a man with a telltale bulge under his jacket. "I've got eyes on a possible courier. Moving to intercept."

She melted into the crowd, her training kicking in as she closed the distance. The man's eyes darted nervously, and Jenna knew she had to act fast.

"All teams," she whispered into her comm, "converge on my position. We may have a lead on the next target."

As she maneuvered through the sea of people, Jenna couldn't help but wonder about the mastermind behind this plot. These rival terrorist groups were playing a dangerous game, and Tel Aviv was caught in the crossfire. With each step, the weight of their mission pressed down on her, the lives of countless innocents hanging in the balance.

Arthur's voice crackled through the earpiece, "Jose, Ali, we've got a confirmed location. Parked vehicle on Allenby Street, silver sedan. Move in, but stay alert."

Jose's muscles tensed as he approached the car, his eyes scanning for any sign of a trigger or observers. "Copy that, Arthur. I see it. Ali, cover my six."

Ali nodded silently, his gaze sweeping the area as Jose crouched beside the vehicle. The bustling street seemed oblivious to the danger lurking mere feet away.

Jose's hands worked deftly, popping the trunk with practiced ease. "We're in. Christ, it's a nasty piece of work."

Inside, a maze of wires and explosives greeted them. Jose's mind raced, analyzing the setup. "Arthur, we've got about ten minutes before this thing goes hot. I can disarm it, but it'll be close."

As Jose began the delicate process of defusing, Ali's voice cut in, low and urgent. "Jose, we've got company. Two men, approaching fast from the north."

Jose's hands didn't falter, but sweat beaded on his brow. "Keep them off me. I need three more minutes."

Across town, Arthur led his team through the crowded marketplace, every sense on high alert. The bomb could be anywhere – in a vendor's cart, beneath a bench, or even carried by an unsuspecting civilian.

"Fan out," Arthur commanded, his voice tight. "Eyes open, people. We're looking for anything out of place."

As they dispersed, Arthur's mind whirled with possibilities. The marketplace was a nightmare scenario – too many people, too many potential hiding spots. One wrong move could trigger a panic, or worse, detonate the bomb prematurely.

A child's laughter caught his attention, and Arthur's chest tightened. So many innocent lives at stake. He pushed the thought aside, focusing on the mission. They had to find that bomb, and fast.

The crackle of static in Jose's earpiece nearly made him jump. He steadied his hand, carefully manipulating the wire cutters around a particularly nasty-looking trigger mechanism.

"Status report," Arthur's voice came through, tense and clipped.

Jose took a measured breath. "It's rigged with a mercury switch. If we so much as jostle this thing, we're toast. I need—"

A burst of gunfire erupted outside, cutting him off. Ali's voice, breathless: "Hostiles engaging! We're pinned down!"

Jose's mind raced. The bomb, the gunfight—everything was unraveling. He gritted his teeth, focusing on the tangle of wires before him. "Arthur, we need backup. Now."

"Negative," Arthur replied, frustration evident. "We've got our own situation brewing. Local cell's mobilizing. They know we're here."

A bead of sweat trickled down Jose's temple. He blinked it away, refusing to let his concentration waver. "Any bright ideas on how to neutralize this thing without moving it?"

THE EXTRACTION

"Work the problem, Jose," Arthur said, his tone softening slightly. "You've got this."

Jose's fingers hovered over the wires, his training battling against the growing pressure. 'Think,' he commanded himself. 'There's always a way.'

Suddenly, an idea struck. It was risky, but their options were dwindling by the second. "I've got a plan," he announced. "But you're not gonna like it."

Jose's hands moved with practiced precision, his fingers dancing around the bomb's intricate wiring. "I'm going to freeze the mercury switch," he explained, voice low and focused. "It'll buy us time to move this thing without triggering it."

"With what?" Arthur's voice crackled through the comm. "We didn't exactly pack a portable freezer."

A wry smile tugged at Jose's lips. "No, but I've got a can of compressed air in my kit. If I spray it upside down, it'll come out as a liquid. Cold enough to do the job."

Outside, the gunfire intensified. Ali's voice cut through the chaos: "Whatever you're doing, do it fast! We can't hold them off much longer!"

Jose pulled out the can, his heart hammering. This was a long shot, but it was all they had. He carefully tilted the bomb, positioning the mercury switch. "Here goes nothing," he muttered.

As he sprayed the freezing liquid, Jose's mind raced through contingencies. If this worked, they'd still need to move fast. If it didn't...

"Jose!" Arthur's urgent voice interrupted his thoughts. "We've got intel on two more devices. Clock's ticking."

Jose felt the weight of lives in his hands. "Almost there," he breathed, watching the mercury solidify. "Just a few more seconds."

The building shook with a nearby explosion. Ali's panicked voice: "They're breaching the perimeter!"

Jose steeled himself. It was now or never. "Alright," he announced, carefully lifting the bomb. "We're mobile. Moving to the extraction point now."

THE EXTRACTION

As he navigated through the chaos, bomb cradled in his arms, Jose couldn't shake the feeling that this was just the beginning. The real test was yet to come.

Arthur's voice crackled through the earpiece, terse and urgent. "Final device located. Heavily guarded warehouse on Hayarkon Street. All teams converge."

Jose cradled the defused bomb, his muscles taut with tension. "Copy that. En route."

The team regrouped in a narrow alley, a block away from the target. Virginia's eyes darted between them, her face a mask of cool determination. "We've got one shot at this. Failure isn't an option."

Arthur nodded, his weathered features set in grim resolve. "Jose, Ali - you're on bomb disposal. Virginia and I will create a diversion and neutralize the guards. Questions?"

Ali's piercing gaze swept over the group. "And if the diversion fails?"

"It won't," Arthur replied, his tone brooking no argument.

As they moved into position, Jose felt a hand on his shoulder. He turned to see Virginia, her blue eyes intense. "Be careful in there," she murmured. "We need that steady hand of yours."

Jose nodded, swallowing hard. "Always am."

The next few moments were a blur of action. Arthur and Virginia's coordinated assault drew the guards away, leaving a narrow window of opportunity. Jose and Ali slipped inside, their footsteps echoing in the cavernous space.

"There," Ali hissed, pointing to a nondescript crate in the corner.

Jose's heart pounded as they approached. He could hear the faint ticking, growing louder with each step. "Cover me," he whispered, kneeling beside the crate.

As he worked to disarm the device, sweat beading on his brow, Ali's voice cut through his concentration. "We've got company. Hurry."

Jose's fingers moved with practiced precision, but doubt gnawed at him. This bomb was different, more complex. "I need more time," he muttered.

THE EXTRACTION

"We don't have it," Ali snapped, raising his weapon.

The warehouse erupted in gunfire. Jose forced himself to focus, blocking out the chaos. His mind raced through possibilities, discarding each one. Time was slipping away.

Suddenly, a memory surfaced - a technique he'd learned years ago, risky but effective. Without hesitation, he made his choice.

"Ali!" he shouted over the din. "I need your belt!"

Ali's eyes widened in surprise, but he complied without question.

With seconds to spare, Jose implemented his desperate plan. The ticking stopped, and for a moment, the world held its breath.

Then, silence.

Jose exhaled shakily, relief washing over him. "It's done," he breathed. "We did it."

As the gunfire outside subsided, Jose couldn't shake the feeling that while they'd won this battle, the war was far from over. The weight of what they'd accomplished - and what still lay ahead - settled heavily on his shoulders.

The Tel Aviv sun beat down mercilessly as Arthur Duggins leaned against a weathered stone wall, his piercing eyes scanning the faces of his team. They had regrouped in a secluded courtyard, the chaos of the city muffled by ancient walls.

"We did it," Arthur said, his voice low and gravelly. "Tel Aviv is safe, for now."

Jose Beals nodded, his jaw clenched tight. "Yeah, but at what cost?" He flexed his hands, still trembling slightly from the tension of defusing that final bomb.

Arthur studied Jose, noting the haunted look in his eyes. "Every life we saved today was worth it," he said firmly.

Raven Blackwood materialized from the shadows, their face an unreadable mask. "The question is, what's our next move? This was just one battle in a much larger war."

Arthur's mind raced, weighing their options. The mission had taken its toll, both physically and mentally. He could see the exhaustion etched on every face.

THE EXTRACTION

"First, we rest," Arthur decided. "We're no good to anyone if we're running on fumes."

Jose snorted, a bitter edge to his voice. "Rest? After what we just saw? After what we just did?"

Arthur placed a hand on Jose's shoulder, feeling the tension thrumming through his friend's body. "I know it's not easy," he said softly. "But we need to process this, all of us."

Raven's eyes narrowed slightly. "Processing can wait. We need to capitalize on this victory, gather intelligence while the enemy is still reeling."

Arthur shook his head. "No, Raven. We push too hard now, we'll make mistakes. Dangerous ones."

As he spoke, Arthur couldn't shake the image of that final bomb, the wire Jose had cut with trembling fingers. They had come so close to failure, to catastrophe. The weight of responsibility pressed down on him, threatening to crush his spirit.

"We saved lives today," Arthur said, as much to himself as to his team. "Remember that. Hold onto it."

Jose's eyes met Arthur's, a flicker of understanding passing between them. "It doesn't make the nightmares go away," Jose murmured.

"No," Arthur agreed. "But it gives us a reason to face them."

As the team fell into a contemplative silence, Arthur allowed himself a moment of quiet pride. They had faced impossible odds and emerged victorious. But the cost of that victory was etched in the lines of worry on their faces, in the shadows behind their eyes.

The war wasn't over. But for now, in this moment of hard-won peace, they had earned their respite. Arthur only hoped it would be enough to prepare them for the battles yet to come.

CHAPTER 17

The acrid smell of smoke lingered in Arthur Duggins' nostrils as he surveyed the bustling Tel Aviv marketplace. His team's successful disarming of the previous bombs had come at a cost – lives lost, injuries sustained. But there was no time for reflection. One final explosive device remained, hidden somewhere in this sea of humanity.

"Eyes sharp, people," Duggins murmured into his comm, his steely gaze scanning the crowd. "Remember, we're looking for anything out of place. A package, a bag, even a misplaced fruit crate."

The chatter of vendors and shoppers filled the air, a stark contrast to the tension coursing through Duggins' body. He counted at least a hundred civilians within immediate blast radius. How many more lives hung in the balance?

"Sir, I've got eyes on a potential target," came a voice through his earpiece. "Northwest corner, near the spice stall."

Duggins' heart rate spiked, but his exterior remained calm. Years of training kicked in as he weaved through the crowd, his hand instinctively brushing against the concealed weapon at his hip.

"Copy that. Maintain visual, but do not approach. I repeat, do not approach."

As he moved, Duggins' mind raced. The previous bombs had been intricately wired, each with its own unique trigger mechanism. What nasty surprise awaited them this time?

He spotted the spice stall, its vibrant colors a mockery of the danger that lurked nearby. His eyes darted around, searching for anything amiss. Then he saw it – a nondescript duffel bag partially hidden behind a stack of crates.

"Possible package identified," Duggins whispered, his voice barely audible above the market din. "Team, converge on my position. Quietly. We can't afford to cause a panic."

As his team members acknowledged, Duggins felt the familiar weight of responsibility settle on his shoulders. One wrong move, one miscalculation, and this vibrant marketplace would become a scene of carnage and devastation.

"Sir," said one of his team members as they approached, "should we begin evacuation procedures?"

Duggins shook his head, his eyes never leaving the suspicious bag. "Negative. A mass exodus could trigger the device. We do this quiet and clean."

He took a deep breath, steeling himself for what came next. The fate of countless innocent lives rested in their hands. Failure was not an option.

Duggins surveyed his team, each member's face a mask of tense focus. He spoke in low, measured tones, his words clipped and precise.

"Alright, listen up. We're splitting into three units. Alpha team, you're with me on the package. Bravo, establish a perimeter - subtle, blend with the crowd. Charlie, start a soft evac - no alarms, no panic. Use market staff if you can. Move."

As his team dispersed, Duggins felt a familiar tightness in his chest. Years of experience couldn't dull the edge of moments like these. He pushed the feeling aside, compartmentalizing as he'd been trained.

"Sir," came a whisper in his earpiece. It was Ramirez, one of his most reliable operatives. "I've got eyes on a suspicious individual near the eastern exit. Middle-aged male, keeps checking his watch and scanning the crowd."

Duggins' mind raced. A spotter? Or just an anxious civilian? He couldn't afford to divert resources, but he also couldn't ignore the potential threat.

"Keep tabs, but maintain your position," he replied, his voice a low growl. "If he makes a move, take him down. Quietly."

As he approached the duffel bag, Duggins' senses were on high alert. The cacophony of the marketplace seemed to fade away, leaving only the sound of his own measured breathing and the faint rustle of fabric as he moved.

"Package in sight," he murmured into his comm. "Preparing to—"

A child's laughter cut through his focus. Duggins' head snapped up to see a young boy, no more than six or seven, running towards the duffel bag, a toy plane held high in his hand.

In that moment, time seemed to slow. Duggins knew he had mere seconds to act before the child inadvertently triggered what could be a catastrophic explosion.

Duggins reacted instinctively, his body moving before his mind could fully process the situation. With a swift, fluid motion, he intercepted the child, scooping him up in one arm while simultaneously positioning himself between the boy and the potential explosive.

"Whoa there, little man," Duggins said, his voice firm but gentle. "This area's off-limits. Let's find your parents, shall we?" He scanned the crowd, heart pounding, acutely aware of every second ticking by.

A frantic woman emerged from the throng, relief washing over her face as she spotted her son. Duggins quickly handed the child over, his mind already refocusing on the task at hand.

"Thompson," he barked into his comm, "I need that disposal kit now. Double time."

Turning back to the duffel bag, Duggins took a deep breath, steadying himself. Years of training kicked in as he approached, each step measured and deliberate. The noise of the marketplace faded to a dull roar in his ears, his senses hyper-focused on the potential threat before him.

Kneeling beside the bag, Duggins carefully unzipped it, revealing a mess of wires and circuitry. His stomach tightened as his eyes locked onto a digital display. 05:47... 05:46... 05:45...

"Christ," he muttered under his breath. The complexity of the device was unlike anything he'd encountered before. This wasn't the work of amateurs.

As he examined the intricate wiring, Duggins' mind raced through possible disarming sequences. Each wire, each connection could be the key to saving countless lives – or ending them in an instant.

"Talk to me, Duggins," came the voice of his second-in-command, Carter, through the earpiece.

"It's a nasty piece of work," Duggins replied, his voice taut with concentration. "Multiple redundancies, pressure sensors... whoever built this wasn't taking any chances."

04:59... 04:58... 04:57...

Sweat beaded on Duggins' forehead as he continued his assessment. He knew the clock was ticking, but rushing could be just as deadly as hesitation. Every decision, every movement had to be perfect.

"Kit's here, sir," Carter announced, sliding the bomb disposal kit toward Duggins.

THE EXTRACTION

Duggins nodded, his eyes never leaving the device. "Good. Listen carefully. We're going to do this by the book, but we need to move fast."

He began guiding Carter through the process, his voice low and measured. "Start by cutting the blue wire on the left. Steady hands, now."

Carter's fingers trembled slightly as he followed the instruction. Duggins felt a twinge of concern but pushed it aside. There was no room for doubt now.

"Good. Now, carefully disconnect the red and green wires from the circuit board."

As they worked, Duggins' mind raced. This bomb was far more sophisticated than intel had suggested. Who were they really dealing with?

03:21... 03:20... 03:19...

"Sir," Carter whispered, "I think I see-"

The air suddenly erupted with the crack of gunfire and panicked screams. Duggins' head snapped up, years of combat experience kicking in instantly.

"Cover!" he barked, grabbing Carter and pulling him behind a nearby stall. The half-disarmed bomb lay exposed, mere feet away.

Duggins' heart pounded as he assessed the situation. Armed men were pouring into the marketplace, their weapons blazing indiscriminately.

"Damn it," he thought, his mind racing. "We were so close. How did they know?"

He locked eyes with Carter, seeing the same mix of frustration and determination reflected back at him. They both knew what was at stake.

"We need to neutralize the threat and get back to that bomb," Duggins said, his voice barely audible over the chaos. "Are you with me?"

Carter nodded grimly. "Always, sir."

THE EXTRACTION

As they prepared to engage, Duggins couldn't shake a nagging feeling. This was more than just a terrorist attack. Something bigger was at play, and they were caught right in the middle of it.

Duggins signaled to his team, their practiced movements a testament to countless operations together. "Carter, Mitchell - flank left. Reyes, with me. Civilians are priority."

The marketplace erupted into a war zone. Duggins moved with precision, his weapon an extension of himself. Each shot found its mark, dropping terrorists with ruthless efficiency.

"Sir, three hostiles, two o'clock!" Reyes shouted over the chaos.

Duggins pivoted, his mind calm despite the adrenaline surge. Two quick bursts, and the threats were neutralized. "Clear!"

As they advanced, Duggins' gaze swept the area, cataloging every detail. Overturned carts, shattered glass, terrified civilians huddled behind whatever cover they could find. His jaw clenched, a familiar anger rising within him.

"These bastards," he thought, "playing with innocent lives like they're expendable."

A child's cry pierced the air. Without hesitation, Duggins sprinted towards the sound, Reyes covering him. He scooped up the boy, shielding him with his body as bullets whizzed past.

"It's okay, son," he murmured, depositing the child behind a sturdy wall. "Stay low, stay quiet."

Returning to the fray, Duggins saw Carter take a glancing hit. "Carter, status!"

"I'm good, sir," came the strained reply. "Just a scratch."

The firefight intensified, but Duggins could sense the tide turning. His team was a well-oiled machine, each member anticipating the others' moves.

As the last terrorist fell, an eerie silence descended. Duggins surveyed the scene, his breath coming in controlled bursts.

"All clear," Mitchell reported. "But sir, the bomb-"

"On it," Duggins replied, already moving. They had mere minutes left. As he knelt beside the device, his hands steady despite the residual adrenaline, a chilling thought crossed his mind.

"This was too coordinated," he mused, carefully reconnecting wires. "They knew exactly when to hit us. We've got a leak somewhere, and when this is over, I'm going to find out who."

Duggins' eyes narrowed as he studied the bomb's intricate wiring, his mind racing against the ticking clock. The digital display flashed 00:30, each second feeling like an eternity.

"Reyes, wire cutters," he commanded, his voice steady despite the pressure.

As Reyes handed him the tool, Duggins muttered, "Red, blue, or yellow. One saves lives, two end them."

His fingers hovered over the wires, muscle memory from countless simulations guiding him. But this was no drill. One wrong move and Tel Aviv would become a graveyard.

"Sir," Carter's voice cracked, "fifteen seconds."

Duggins took a deep breath, pushing aside the weight of thousands of lives. He focused on the bomb's design, searching for that telltale sign...

There. A subtle difference in the casing.

"Not today," he growled, snipping the yellow wire with three seconds to spare.

The timer froze. For a moment, no one dared breathe.

Then, silence. Beautiful, life-affirming silence.

Duggins exhaled slowly, allowing himself a rare smile. "It's done. We did it, team."

A collective sigh of relief swept through the marketplace. Mitchell clapped Duggins on the shoulder, his usual stoicism replaced by a grin.

"Never doubted you for a second, boss."

Duggins nodded, the enormity of what they'd accomplished washing over him. "We saved a lot of lives today. Remember this moment. It's why we do what we do."

THE EXTRACTION

As the team gathered around, their faces a mix of exhaustion and elation, Duggins felt a familiar pang. They'd won this battle, but the war was far from over.

"Alright, people," he said, his voice tinged with both pride and caution. "Let's secure the area and prepare for debrief. Our job's not done yet."

The adrenaline-fueled high began to ebb, leaving behind a bone-deep weariness that seemed to seep into every fiber of their beings. Duggins watched his team slump against nearby market stalls, their faces etched with the weight of their ordeal.

Carter, the youngest of the group, slid down to sit on the dusty ground, her hands trembling slightly. "I can't believe we... we almost..."

"But we didn't," Duggins interjected firmly, his piercing gaze sweeping over his team. He felt the familiar tightness in his chest, the burden of command pressing down on him. "We succeeded. Remember that."

Mitchell nodded wearily, his usual stoic demeanor cracking to reveal the toll of their mission. "It was close, Arthur. Too damn close."

Duggins approached his second-in-command, placing a steady hand on his shoulder. "It always is, old friend. That's the nature of what we do."

He took a moment to gather his thoughts, acutely aware of the exhausted eyes fixed upon him. The marketplace around them was eerily quiet, the aftermath of their firefight still hanging in the air.

"Listen up, team," Duggins began, his voice low but commanding. "What we accomplished here today... it's why we put on this uniform. Why we make the sacrifices we do."

He paused, allowing his words to sink in. "We saved lives today. Hundreds, maybe thousands. People who will never know how close they came to oblivion."

Carter looked up, her eyes glistening. "But at what cost, sir? We lost Johnson and Reeves..."

Duggins felt the familiar stab of grief, but pushed it aside. "We honor their sacrifice by continuing our mission. By ensuring their loss wasn't in vain."

THE EXTRACTION

He surveyed his team, noting the mix of exhaustion and determination on their faces. "Take a moment. Breathe. Remember why we're here. Then we move out and face what comes next."

As his team gathered themselves, Duggins turned away, his mind already racing ahead to the challenges that awaited them. The mission was over, but the real work was just beginning.

Duggins stood at the edge of the marketplace, his eyes scanning the horizon as sirens wailed in the distance. The adrenaline was wearing off, leaving a gnawing uncertainty in its wake.

"Sir," Agent Simmons approached, her voice barely above a whisper. "Local authorities are five minutes out. What's our play?"

Duggins turned, his weathered features set in a grim mask. "We stick to protocol. Minimal engagement, no names. Let me do the talking."

As he spoke, he caught a glimpse of his reflection in a shattered storefront window. The man staring back looked older, more haggard than he remembered.

"Arthur," Simmons pressed, using his first name – a rarity that spoke volumes about the gravity of the situation. "What about Johnson and Reeves? Their families..."

Duggins felt a tightness in his chest. "I'll handle it personally. It's the least I can do."

He turned back to the team, noting the mix of exhaustion and apprehension on their faces. The weight of command had never felt heavier.

"Listen up," he began, his voice low but firm. "What happened here... it's going to have repercussions. Political, personal... hell, probably some we can't even anticipate yet."

Agent Carter stepped forward, her eyes narrowed. "You think we'll be scapegoated?"

Duggins shook his head. "I don't know. But whatever comes, we face it together. We did our job. We saved lives. Remember that."

As the first police vehicles screeched into the square, Duggins straightened his shoulders. The immediate threat was neutralized, but he couldn't shake the feeling that this was just the beginning of a much longer, darker road.

CHAPTER 18

The abandoned warehouse loomed before them, its rusted metal exterior a stark contrast to the high-tech operation they'd just barely escaped. Arthur Duggins led his team through the heavy steel door, his piercing eyes scanning every shadow for potential threats.

"Clear," he growled, his voice low and tense. The team spread out, securing exits and vantage points with practiced efficiency.

Duggins' jaw clenched as he spotted Virginia Turner across the room, her tailored suit pristine despite the chaos of the past few hours. His blood boiled at the sight of her composed demeanor.

"Turner!" he barked, striding towards her with purpose. "What the hell happened out there?"

Virginia turned, her blue eyes cool and assessing. "Agent Duggins, I'm glad to see you made it—"

"Cut the crap," Duggins interrupted, closing the distance between them. "We were compromised. Our position was leaked. I want answers, and I want them now."

His mind raced, replaying the ambush that had nearly cost them everything. The intel had been perfect, but the enemy had been waiting. Someone had to have tipped them off.

Virginia's eyebrow arched slightly. "I understand you're upset, Arthur, but accusations won't—"

"This isn't about being upset," Duggins snapped, his voice low and dangerous. "This is about a double-cross that nearly got my entire team killed. Start talking, or I'll start assuming you're the one responsible."

He watched her carefully, years of experience allowing him to catch the slight tightening around her eyes, the almost imperceptible shift in her stance. She was hiding something.

"You're out of line, Agent," Virginia said, her tone sharpening. "I coordinated this operation with the utmost—"

Duggins cut her off again, stepping closer. "The utmost what, Turner? Precision? Care? Because from where I'm standing, it looks like someone sold us out. And you're the one with all the strings."

He could feel the tension radiating from his team, their eyes darting between him and Virginia. They trusted him, followed his lead without question. But this confrontation could shatter everything if he was wrong.

Virginia's composure slipped for just a moment, a flash of something – fear? anger? – crossing her face before she regained control. "I suggest you calm down and think very carefully about what you're implying, Arthur."

Duggins didn't back down, his voice a low growl. "Oh, I'm thinking plenty clearly. And right now, I'm thinking you've got about thirty seconds to start explaining before I consider you a hostile threat to this operation."

His hand twitched, inches away from his sidearm. The warehouse felt charged with electricity, every breath, every movement amplified in the tense silence.

Virginia's eyes narrowed, calculating. "You're making a mistake, Duggins. One you can't come back from."

"Maybe," he replied, his gaze unwavering. "But I'd rather make that mistake than let a traitor walk free. Last chance, Turner. What really happened out there?"

Virginia's carefully constructed facade began to crumble under Duggins' relentless pressure. Her eyes darted nervously around the warehouse, seeking an escape that didn't exist.

"You're... you're delusional, Arthur," she stammered, her usual eloquence faltering. "The mission parameters were clear. If something went wrong, it wasn't on my end."

Duggins took another step forward, his voice low and dangerous. "Cut the bullshit, Virginia. I've known you long enough to spot when you're lying. And right now? You're practically screaming it."

He watched as beads of sweat formed on her brow, her perfectly manicured nails digging into her palms. The composed intelligence coordinator was unraveling before his eyes.

"You don't understand the pressure I'm under," Virginia hissed, her tone shifting from defensive to desperate. "The things I've had to do to keep us all safe, to maintain our position..."

Duggins' mind raced, piecing together the implications. "So you did sell us out. But to whom? And why?"

THE EXTRACTION

Virginia's laugh was bitter, tinged with hysteria. "You think it's that simple? That there are clear sides in this game we play? Oh, Arthur. You've always been so... honorable. So naive."

The warehouse seemed to close in around them, the air thick with tension. Duggins could feel his team shifting behind him, ready to act at a moment's notice. But this was his fight, his responsibility.

"Then enlighten me, Virginia," he growled, his patience wearing dangerously thin. "Because right now, all I see is a traitor who's put my team - my family - in danger. And that's something I can't forgive."

Duggins took another step forward, his eyes never leaving Virginia's face. The weight of betrayal sat heavy in his chest, fueling a righteous anger that threatened to consume him. "You're going to tell me everything, Turner. Every dirty little secret, every backroom deal. And then you're going to face justice for what you've done."

Virginia's composure cracked further, her carefully constructed facade crumbling away to reveal the cornered animal beneath. "You don't get to judge me, Arthur," she spat, her voice trembling with a mixture of fear and defiance. "You have no idea what it takes to keep this country safe. The compromises, the sacrifices-"

"Save it," Duggins cut her off, his tone as sharp as a blade. "Your excuses mean nothing to the men and women you've put in harm's way. To the families who've lost loved ones because of your 'compromises.'"

He could see the desperation in her eyes, the frantic calculations behind that piercing blue gaze. Virginia's hand twitched, and Duggins' instincts screamed a warning.

"Don't do it, Virginia," he warned, his body tensing in anticipation. "There's no way out of this. Not anymore."

For a moment, time seemed to stand still. Then, with a speed that belied her years behind a desk, Virginia's hand flew to her hip. The metallic glint of a pistol caught the dim light as she drew her weapon.

"I won't let you destroy everything I've built," she snarled, leveling the gun at Duggins' chest.

In that instant, as adrenaline surged through his veins, Duggins felt an odd sense of clarity. This was it - the moment where all pretenses fell away, where the true nature of their world revealed itself in all its brutal, unforgiving glory.

"So this is how it ends, Virginia?" he asked, his voice steady despite the gun aimed at his heart. "All those years of service, and you throw it away like this?"

Without hesitation, Duggins dove behind a concrete pillar as Virginia's first shot cracked through the air. The bullet chipped the edge of his cover, sending fragments of concrete flying. His heart pounded, but his mind remained razor-sharp.

"You're making a mistake, Turner!" he shouted, drawing his own weapon. He took a deep breath, steadying his aim. "Stand down, and we can end this without bloodshed!"

Virginia's laughter echoed through the cavernous space. "You're a fool, Arthur! There's no going back now!"

Duggins peered around the pillar, squeezing off two rapid shots. The muzzle flash illuminated Virginia's face for a split second, her features twisted with fury. She ducked behind an overturned table, bullets splintering the wood.

"Dammit," Duggins muttered under his breath. He'd hoped to end this quickly, but Turner was proving to be a more formidable opponent than he'd anticipated. Years of desk work hadn't dulled her combat instincts.

The air filled with the deafening roar of gunfire as they exchanged shots. Bullets ricocheted off metal surfaces, creating a deadly symphony that reverberated through the rendezvous point. Duggins' ears rang, but he forced himself to focus, to listen for any telltale sounds of movement.

"You can't win this, Virginia!" he called out, trying to keep her talking, to pinpoint her location. "How long did you think you could keep your dirty dealings hidden?"

"Long enough to secure my future!" she spat back. "You have no idea how deep this goes, Arthur. You're just a pawn in a much larger game!"

As she spoke, Duggins caught a glimpse of movement. He fired instinctively, hearing a sharp cry of pain. Had he hit her? Or was it just a graze? His mind raced, calculating his next move.

"There's nowhere to run," he said, his voice steady despite the chaos around them. "End this now, before more blood is spilled."

Duggins' eyes darted across the room, assessing his surroundings. A metal staircase leading to an elevated walkway caught his attention. If he could reach it, he'd have a clear line of sight over the entire area.

"You're wrong, Arthur," Turner's voice echoed, its usual composure cracking. "There's always somewhere to run."

As she spoke, Duggins made his move. With practiced agility, he sprinted towards the staircase, his footsteps light despite his muscular frame. Bullets whizzed past, missing him by mere inches.

"Dammit, Virginia," he thought, heart pounding. "What turned you into this?"

Reaching the stairs, he took them two at a time, keeping his weapon trained on the area below. The cool metal railing pressed against his palm as he ascended, each step bringing him closer to his vantage point.

"You can't outmaneuver me, Turner!" he shouted, hoping to draw her attention away from his new position. "I've seen your type before. Ambitious, ruthless, willing to sacrifice anything for power."

Turner's laugh was bitter, tinged with desperation. "And what type is that, Arthur? The type that refuses to be a mindless drone? The type that sees the bigger picture?"

As she spoke, Duggins caught a flash of movement. Turner was darting between shipping containers, using them as cover. Her usually immaculate appearance was disheveled, a streak of blood marring her cheek.

"There's no bigger picture that justifies betrayal," Duggins growled, taking aim. But before he could fire, Turner disappeared behind another container, her tactical prowess matching his own.

Duggins pressed his back against the wall, his breath steady despite the adrenaline coursing through his veins. He could hear Turner's movements, calculating, precise - just like her words had always been.

"Betrayal?" Turner's voice echoed from below, a hint of strain breaking through her usually controlled tone. "You don't understand the game we're playing, Arthur."

A burst of gunfire erupted, forcing Duggins to duck. Fragments of concrete rained down around him as bullets chipped away at his cover.

"Then enlighten me," he called out, his voice a mix of anger and determination. He shifted his position, eyes scanning for any sign of movement. "What's worth throwing away everything we've worked for?"

Turner's laugh was hollow. "Everything we've worked for? Wake up, Arthur. We're pawns, expendable assets in a much larger chess game."

THE EXTRACTION

Duggins' jaw clenched, his grip tightening on his weapon. He'd heard similar justifications before, from operatives who'd lost their way. But coming from Turner, it stung more than he cared to admit.

"So that's it?" he asked, inching towards the edge of his cover. "You decided to change the rules?"

Another burst of gunfire answered him, closer this time. Duggins rolled, coming up in a crouch behind a large crate. His eyes narrowed, focusing on a flash of movement to his left.

"The rules were always rigged, Arthur," Turner's voice came, tinged with a mix of frustration and desperation. "I'm just evening the odds."

Duggins took a deep breath, years of training kicking in. He visualized the layout of the warehouse, Turner's likely position, the angles of fire. In his mind, he could see the chessboard Turner spoke of, but he wasn't about to let her dictate the moves.

"Even if that were true," he called out, voice steady, "there are lines we don't cross. People we don't betray."

As he spoke, Duggins made his move, darting from his position to a new vantage point. He caught a glimpse of Turner, her eyes wide with surprise at his sudden appearance.

Their eyes locked for a split second, a moment of unspoken understanding passing between them. Then, the air once again filled with the deafening sound of gunfire as the deadly game continued.

Turner's desperation was palpable as she made her move. Duggins caught a flash of her blonde hair as she darted between stacks of crates, attempting to circle around his position. Her footsteps echoed off the concrete floor, betraying her location.

"You're out of options, Virginia," Duggins called out, his voice steady despite the adrenaline coursing through his veins. He shifted his weight, ready to react. "There's no winning move here."

"That's where you're wrong, Arthur," Turner's voice rang out, closer than he expected. "I always have an ace up my sleeve."

Duggins' instincts screamed danger. He spun, bringing his weapon to bear just as Turner emerged from behind a forklift, her gun aimed squarely at his chest.

Time seemed to slow. Duggins' mind raced, analyzing the situation in microseconds. He recognized the calculated risk in Turner's eyes, the slight tremor in her usually steady hands. She was gambling everything on this moment.

"Don't do this," Duggins warned, his finger tensing on the trigger. "You know how this ends."

But even as he spoke, Duggins was already in motion. He dropped and rolled, feeling the heat of Turner's bullet as it whizzed past his ear. In one fluid motion, he came up behind a stack of metal drums, using them as cover while simultaneously lining up his shot.

Turner's eyes widened in shock as she realized her gambit had failed. Duggins had anticipated her move, countering it with the precision of a seasoned operative. She found herself exposed, caught in the open with nowhere to hide.

"It's over, Virginia," Duggins said, his voice carrying a mix of regret and resolve. "Drop the weapon."

Duggins' piercing eyes locked onto Turner, his aim unwavering. In that split second, he saw a flicker of desperation cross her face, her mask of cool professionalism finally cracking.

"You don't understand, Arthur," Turner pleaded, her voice strained. "I had no choice—"

But Duggins knew better. Years of experience had taught him to recognize the telltale signs of a cornered operative. Turner's fingers tightened on her weapon, her body tensing to spring into action.

Without hesitation, Duggins squeezed the trigger. The crack of the gunshot echoed through the warehouse, followed by an eerie silence.

Turner's eyes widened in shock as the bullet found its mark. Her gun clattered to the floor as she stumbled backward, a crimson stain blossoming on her tailored suit.

Duggins approached cautiously, his weapon still trained on her. "It didn't have to end this way, Virginia," he said, his voice low and filled with a mixture of regret and resolve.

As Turner collapsed to her knees, Duggins felt a pang of sadness. Despite her betrayal, they had once been colleagues, perhaps even friends. But the mission, the greater good, had to come first. It always did in their line of work.

"You... you don't know... what you've done," Turner gasped, her breath coming in ragged bursts.

Duggins knelt beside her, his mind racing. What secrets was she taking to her grave? What larger conspiracy had he just stumbled into?

"Tell me," he urged, but it was too late. Virginia Turner's eyes glazed over, the light fading from them as she slumped to the ground.

Standing up, Duggins surveyed the scene, his jaw clenched. The gun battle was over, but he knew this was just the beginning. Whatever web of deceit Turner had been caught in, he was now irrevocably entangled in it too.

"Rest in peace, Virginia," he muttered, holstering his weapon. "I'll find the truth, whatever it takes."

CHAPTER 19

The jet bridge creaked under Arthur Duggins' weary feet as he stepped onto American soil. The stale airport air hit his nostrils, a stark contrast to the desert heat they'd left behind. His team followed close behind, their exhaustion palpable.

"Eyes sharp," Arthur murmured, his gaze sweeping the terminal. "We're not home free yet."

Jose Beals grunted in acknowledgment, his muscular frame taut with tension. Raven Blackwood glided past, melting effortlessly into the crowd.

Arthur's mind raced, cataloging potential threats. A businessman on his phone? A janitor pushing a cart? Every face held the possibility of danger.

"Baggage claim," he ordered, leading the way through the throng of travelers.

As they walked, Arthur noticed Jose's clenched jaw, the haunted look in his eyes. The mission had taken its toll on all of them, but Jose seemed particularly affected.

"You good?" Arthur asked quietly.

Jose's response was clipped. "Fine, sir."

Arthur knew better than to push. The debriefing would come soon enough.

They reached the baggage carousel, positioning themselves strategically around its circumference. Arthur's fingers twitched, inches from his concealed weapon.

"Sir," Raven's cool voice cut through the din. "Our ride's here."

Arthur followed Raven's gaze to a nondescript man holding a sign with their cover names. He nodded, grateful for the efficiency of their extraction team.

As they moved towards the exit, Arthur couldn't shake the feeling of being watched. His instincts, honed by years in the field, screamed danger.

"Something's off," he muttered to Jose.

Jose's hand moved imperceptibly closer to his own weapon. "Hostiles?"

"Can't be sure. Raven, take point. Jose, watch our six."

The team seamlessly adjusted their formation, years of training kicking in. Arthur's mind raced through contingency plans as they approached the waiting vehicle.

Just as they reached the car, a flash of movement caught Arthur's eye. He spun, positioning himself between the threat and his team.

"Down!" he shouted, drawing his weapon in one fluid motion.

The airport erupted into chaos as the first shots rang out.

Arthur Duggins guided his team through the dimly lit streets of Washington D.C., his piercing eyes constantly scanning for potential threats. The nondescript sedan wound its way through a maze of residential areas, each turn taking them further from the bustling city center.

"We're almost there," Arthur murmured, his voice low and gravelly. "Everyone stay alert."

The car pulled up to an unremarkable brownstone, blending seamlessly with its neighbors. Arthur's hand instinctively moved to his concealed weapon as he exited the vehicle, surveying the quiet street.

"Clear," he announced, motioning for the team to follow.

As they entered the safehouse, Arthur's trained gaze swept the interior, noting exit points and potential defensive positions. The apartment was sparsely furnished, a testament to its utilitarian purpose.

"Home sweet home," Raven muttered sarcastically, dropping her gear by the door.

Arthur watched as his team members shuffled into the living area, their exhaustion palpable. Jose practically collapsed onto a worn leather couch, his head falling back against the cushions with a heavy thud. Raven curled up in an armchair, her usually sharp eyes now heavy-lidded and unfocused.

"Get some rest," Arthur ordered, his own fatigue threatening to overwhelm him. "We'll debrief in a few hours."

As he moved to secure the perimeter, Arthur's mind raced with the implications of their recent mission. The betrayal, the close calls, the lives lost - it all weighed heavily on his conscience. He leaned against the wall, allowing himself a moment of vulnerability away from his team's eyes.

"Sir?" Jose's voice startled him. "You should rest too."

Arthur nodded, grateful for the concern. "Soon. Just need to make sure we're secure."

He returned to the living room, taking in the sight of his battered and bruised team. Despite everything, a surge of pride welled up in his chest. They had made it back alive, against all odds.

As Arthur finally allowed himself to sink into an armchair, he couldn't shake the nagging feeling that their troubles were far from over. The real battle, he feared, was just beginning.

Arthur Duggins straightened his posture, ignoring the protest of his aching muscles. He cleared his throat, the sound cutting through the heavy silence that had settled over the room.

"Alright, team," he began, his voice a mix of exhaustion and resolute determination. "I know we're all beat, but we need to debrief while everything's fresh."

He scanned the faces of his operatives, noting the flicker of reluctance in their eyes. "Let's go around the room. I want honest assessments. What worked, what didn't, how you're feeling. No holding back."

Raven spoke first, her usual crisp tone dulled by fatigue. "The intel was solid, but our exit strategy was compromised. We need better contingencies."

Arthur nodded, making a mental note. "Agreed. We'll address that in future planning."

His gaze shifted to Jose, who was staring at his hands. "Jose?"

The younger agent looked up, his eyes haunted. "I... I keep replaying that moment at the checkpoint. If I'd been faster..."

"You did what you could," Arthur interjected, his voice softening slightly. "We all did."

As each team member shared their thoughts, Arthur felt a complex mix of emotions churning inside him. Relief at their survival warred with regret over the mission's cost. He listened intently, cataloging their concerns and insights for future operations.

When it was his turn to speak, Arthur leaned forward, his piercing eyes meeting each of theirs. "We made it back. That's what matters. But we can't ignore the close calls. We'll learn from this, adapt, and come back stronger."

He paused, allowing his words to sink in. "I'm proud of each of you. Now get some rest. We're not out of the woods yet."

As the team dispersed, Arthur remained in his chair, the weight of command settling heavily on his shoulders. The debrief had confirmed his suspicions – they'd survived this mission, but greater challenges lay ahead. He closed his eyes, steeling himself for whatever came next.

The room fell into a heavy silence as Arthur's words hung in the air. It was Ramirez who broke it first, her voice low and tinged with a mix of pride and sorrow.

"We all knew the risks going in," she said, running a hand through her disheveled hair. "But that moment in the abandoned factory... I've never felt so close to death."

Jackson nodded grimly. "I can still hear the bullets ricocheting off the walls. If it wasn't for Chen's quick thinking with that smoke grenade..."

Chen shrugged, his face a mask of stoicism. "We do what we have to. For the mission. For each other."

Arthur watched as his team recounted their brushes with mortality, each story etching lines of tension across their faces. The sacrifices they'd made were written in the haunted looks in their eyes, the barely-healed wounds on their bodies.

Suddenly, Thompson's fist slammed onto the coffee table, causing everyone to flinch. "And for what?" he snarled, his eyes blazing. "So that bastard Beals could sell us out?"

The tension in the room skyrocketed. Arthur felt his muscles tense, ready to intervene if necessary.

"We don't know that for certain," Chen said carefully, but doubt clouded his voice.

"Don't we?" Thompson retorted. "The intel leak, the ambush... it all points to him."

Ramirez shook her head, conflict evident in her expression. "I can't believe Jose would do that to us. We've been through too much together."

"People change," Jackson muttered darkly. "Money has a way of rewriting loyalties."

As the accusations flew, Arthur's mind raced. He'd trained with Jose, trusted him. The thought of betrayal cut deep, but he couldn't ignore the evidence. Trust, once shattered, was nearly impossible to rebuild in their line of work.

"Enough," Arthur said, his voice cutting through the heated debate. "We'll get to the bottom of this. But right now, we need to focus on..."

Arthur's firm voice cut through the escalating tension like a knife. "We can't let this divide us," he said, his piercing gaze sweeping across the room. "Unity is our strength. It's what's kept us alive this long."

The team fell silent, their anger momentarily subdued by the quiet authority in Arthur's words. He leaned forward, elbows on his knees, his weathered face a map of hard-earned wisdom.

"Beals will answer for his actions, if he's guilty," Arthur continued. "But right now, we need to focus on healing and moving forward. This mission... it took a toll on all of us."

Thompson's jaw clenched, but he nodded reluctantly. "You're right, boss. It's just... hard to swallow."

Arthur felt a twinge in his left shoulder, a reminder of a close call during the extraction. He rubbed it absently, his mind drifting to the moments of sheer terror they'd all faced.

"We've all got scars from this one," he said softly. "Some you can see, some you can't. It's time we acknowledged that."

Chen cleared his throat, his usual stoic demeanor cracking. "I... I keep hearing the explosion in my dreams," he admitted, his voice barely above a whisper. "I see Martinez's face right before..."

The room grew heavy with shared grief. Arthur watched as his team, hardened operatives all, began to let their guards down.

Ramirez hugged herself tightly. "I thought we were done for in that alley," she said. "I've never felt so... helpless."

One by one, they opened up, sharing fears and doubts that had been buried beneath layers of training and bravado. Arthur listened intently, his heart aching for his team even as he wrestled with his own demons.

"The weight of command," he thought, "never gets easier to bear."

As the confessions flowed, a palpable shift occurred in the room. Thompson reached out, gripping Chen's shoulder firmly. "We made it through, brother. Together."

Ramirez wiped a tear, her voice stronger as she added, "That's right. We've got each other's backs, always have."

Arthur watched as his team drew closer, both physically and emotionally. The invisible barriers that often separated them in the field dissolved, replaced by a raw, unspoken understanding.

"This is what makes us unbreakable," he thought, a surge of pride warming his chest.

Clearing his throat, Arthur stood, drawing all eyes to him. "Listen up, team," he began, his voice low but unwavering. "What we've been through... it's the stuff of nightmares. But look around you. We're still here, still fighting."

He paced slowly, making eye contact with each member. "Our mission isn't over. The world out there? It's counting on us, even if it doesn't know it. We carry that weight so others don't have to."

Arthur paused, his piercing gaze sweeping the room. "But we don't carry it alone. This team, this family we've forged in fire and blood, it's our strength. Our shield against the darkness."

He clenched his fist, emphasizing each word. "We will honor those we've lost by pushing forward. By standing tall in the face of evil and saying, 'Not on our watch.'"

The room crackled with renewed energy, faces set with determination. Arthur allowed himself a small smile, knowing they were ready for whatever came next.

"Rest up," he ordered. "Tomorrow, we get back to work. The fight for justice never ends, and neither do we."

As Arthur's final words hung in the air, the team members began to disperse, their movements sluggish with exhaustion. Rodriguez, the team's sharpshooter, stumbled slightly as he rose, catching himself on the arm of the couch. "Christ, I'm beat," he muttered, rubbing his eyes.

"Get some shut-eye, all of you," Arthur commanded, his tone softening. "You've earned it."

One by one, they shuffled out, exchanging weary nods and clasped shoulders. The sound of doors clicking shut echoed through the safehouse, leaving Arthur alone in the dimly lit living room.

He sank into the worn leather armchair, his body protesting every movement. The remote felt heavy in his hand as he flicked on the television, bathing the room in a flickering blue glow.

"...tensions continue to rise in the Middle East as..." The newscaster's voice faded into background noise as Arthur's mind raced, replaying the mission's critical moments.

"Dammit, Beals," he whispered, his jaw clenching. The betrayal still stung, a raw wound that threatened to fester. "How did I miss the signs?"

Arthur's gaze drifted to the window, watching shadows dance across the curtains. The weight of command pressed down on him, heavier than ever.

"What's our next move?" he mused, his fingers drumming a restless rhythm on the armrest. "They'll be gunning for us now. We need to stay three steps ahead."

The TV droned on, images of conflict flashing across the screen. Arthur's eyes narrowed, recognizing terrain they'd traversed mere days ago.

"It never ends," he thought, a mixture of weariness and determination coursing through him. "But neither do we."

As the news segment shifted to a story about unrest in Eastern Europe, Arthur's phone buzzed on the coffee table. He snatched it up, his exhaustion momentarily forgotten as he recognized the encrypted message from his handler.

"Already?" he muttered, quickly decoding the text. His eyes widened as he absorbed the information.

Arthur stood abruptly, his muscles protesting the sudden movement. He strode to the hallway, hesitating for a moment before rapping his knuckles against the first door.

"Team, we've got a situation," he called out, his voice low but urgent. "Living room, five minutes."

As doors creaked open and groggy faces emerged, Arthur returned to the living room, his mind racing. He paced, formulating a plan as his team assembled.

"What's the word, boss?" asked a bleary-eyed operative, stifling a yawn.

Arthur took a deep breath, his posture straightening as he addressed the room. "I know you're all exhausted, but duty calls. We've got credible intel on Ali Shabaab's whereabouts."

A ripple of tension coursed through the room. Arthur continued, his voice tinged with a mix of determination and concern, "He's been spotted in Belgrade. We have a 48-hour window to intercept before he goes to ground again."

"Belgrade?" one team member groaned. "We just got back."

Arthur's eyes hardened. "I know. But this is our chance to finally nail that bastard. We can't let it slip away."

As he scanned the faces of his team, Arthur saw the fatigue in their eyes begin to give way to resolve. They knew the stakes, understood the importance of their mission.

"Wheels up in three hours," Arthur announced, his tone brooking no argument. "Gear up, rest if you can. This one's going to be tough."

As the team dispersed to prepare, Arthur felt a familiar surge of adrenaline coursing through his veins. The weariness of moments ago was replaced by a sharp focus, his mind already plotting their approach.

"Back into the shadows," he thought, a grim smile playing at the corners of his mouth. "Let's hope we all make it out this time."

CHAPTER 20

The fluorescent lights flickered overhead, casting harsh shadows across the faces of the C.O.R.E. team. Arthur Duggins scanned the room, his piercing gaze taking in the slumped shoulders and dark-ringed eyes of his operatives. The air hung heavy with the acrid smell of stale coffee and sweat.

Duggins cleared his throat, breaking the tense silence. "Listen up, people. I know we're all running on fumes here, but we've got work to do."

He stood, his imposing frame commanding attention despite the weariness etched into every line of his face. The chair scraped against the concrete floor, echoing in the cramped space.

"What we accomplished in Sarajevo..." Duggins paused, allowing the weight of their recent mission to settle. "It wasn't pretty, but it was necessary. Each of you pushed yourselves to the limit, and then some."

His mind flashed to the firefight in the abandoned warehouse, the smell of gunpowder and blood still fresh in his memory. He pushed the image aside, focusing on the present.

"I won't sugarcoat it. We lost good people out there." Duggins' voice dropped, a hint of emotion creeping in. "But their sacrifice wasn't in vain. The intel we secured has already prevented three potential attacks on US soil."

He locked eyes with each team member, noting the mix of pride and exhaustion in their expressions. These were the best of the best, and they'd been through hell together.

"I know you're tired. I know you're hurting. But what we do..." Duggins clenched his fist, emphasizing each word. "What we do matters. We're the thin line between chaos and order, between justice and anarchy."

A low murmur of agreement rippled through the room. Duggins felt a surge of pride in his chest, tempered by the weight of responsibility on his shoulders.

"Our fight isn't over. The world out there?" He jerked his thumb towards the door. "It's getting more dangerous by the day. We're the ones who stand in the gap, who do what others can't or won't."

Duggins paused, letting his words sink in. He could see the spark of determination reigniting in his team's eyes, pushing back against the fatigue.

"So take a moment. Remember why we do this. Remember the lives we've saved, the disasters we've averted. Because in a few minutes, we're going to get our next assignment, and I need every one of you at your best."

He sat back down, the chair creaking under his weight. As the room fell into a contemplative silence, Duggins allowed himself a brief moment of vulnerability. How many more missions could they endure? How many more sacrifices would be demanded of them?

But as quickly as the doubts surfaced, he pushed them aside. This was the life he'd chosen, the burden he'd accepted. And as long as there were threats to face and innocents to protect, Arthur Duggins and his team would be there, standing on the front lines of a war few would ever know about.

The door swung open with a soft hiss, cutting through the tense silence. A tall, austere woman strode in, her crisp navy suit a stark contrast to the team's battle-worn attire. Duggins recognized her immediately - Director Caroline Hawthorne, head of covert operations.

"Team," Duggins said, standing to attention. "Director Hawthorne."

Hawthorne's steely gaze swept the room, her lips pursed in a thin line. "At ease," she commanded, her voice clipped. "I'll cut to the chase. We've intercepted chatter about a potential bioweapon exchange in Bucharest. Details are scarce, but the implications are... concerning."

Duggins felt his pulse quicken. Bioweapons meant catastrophic civilian casualties. "Timeline?" he asked, his mind already racing through logistics.

"72 hours," Hawthorne replied, sliding a thin folder across the table. "This contains all we know. It's not much, but it's all you've got. Questions?"

Jose Beals leaned forward, his brow furrowed. "Extraction plan?"

"Minimal support available. You'll be largely on your own," Hawthorne said, her tone leaving no room for argument.

As the director continued her brief, Duggins watched his team. The exhaustion in their eyes was slowly being replaced by a familiar intensity. They knew the stakes.

After Hawthorne left, a heavy silence settled over the room. It was Raven who broke it, her voice uncharacteristically soft. "Well, that was... illuminating."

Jose snorted, rubbing his face. "Illuminating? More like a black hole of information. How are we supposed to pull this off with so little to go on?"

Duggins understood their frustration. He felt it too, coupled with a bone-deep weariness that threatened to overwhelm him. But they didn't have the luxury of rest or self-pity.

"We've done more with less," he reminded them, his voice steady despite the turmoil in his gut. "Remember Sarajevo?"

A collective groan went up, followed by a few chuckles. The mission in Sarajevo had been a nightmare, but they'd pulled through. Together.

"God, don't remind me," Jose said, shaking his head. "I still have nightmares about those tunnels."

Raven's lips quirked in a rare smile. "At least this time we're not starting with a compromised cover and a malfunctioning comm system."

As they continued to reminisce, Duggins observed the subtle shift in the room's atmosphere. The shared memories, both good and bad, were reminding them of what they were capable of as a unit. The trust that had been strained during their last mission was slowly knitting itself back together.

But beneath the banter, Duggins could see the toll their work had taken. The dark circles under Jose's eyes, the slight tremor in Raven's usually steady hands, the way each of them seemed to be running on nothing but sheer willpower and caffeine.

He cleared his throat, drawing their attention. "I know we're all running on fumes here," he said, meeting each of their gazes in turn. "But what we do... it matters. Those people in Bucharest? They're counting on us, even if they don't know it."

Duggins paused, feeling the weight of his next words. "We've been through hell together. We've seen the worst this job can throw at us. But we're still here. Still fighting. That's not nothing."

He saw the impact of his words reflected in their eyes - a rekindling of purpose, a steeling of resolve. They were battered, exhausted, pushed to their limits. But they weren't broken. Not yet.

"Now," Duggins said, reaching for the folder Hawthorne had left, "let's figure out how to save the world. Again."

The storage room buzzed with activity as Duggins' team moved with practiced efficiency, gathering their gear. Arthur watched as Raven meticulously checked her communications equipment, her fingers flying over the devices with precision despite her earlier tremor.

"Raven," Duggins called, striding over. "Make sure we've got backup uplinks this time. Can't afford another Bucharest situation."

She nodded, jaw clenching at the memory. "Already on it, boss. Triple redundancy."

Across the room, Jose was loading up on tactical gear, his movements slower than usual. Duggins frowned, concern gnawing at him. "You good, Jose?"

"Just peachy, Duggins," Jose replied, forcing a grin that didn't reach his eyes. "Nothing a few more cups of coffee won't fix."

Arthur's mind raced, weighing the risks. *We're not at a hundred percent, but we don't have a choice. The mission won't wait.*

"Alright, team," he announced, his voice cutting through the clatter of equipment. "Gear up, then hit the simulators. I want everyone sharp before we move out."

As the team dispersed, Duggins made his way to the tech lab. Dr. Eliza Chen, their resident gadget guru, was hunched over a workbench, her dark hair pulled back in a messy bun.

"Doc," Arthur greeted, "what've you got for us?"

Eliza straightened, revealing bloodshot eyes behind her glasses. "Duggins. I've been working on something special for this one." She held up a sleek, pen-like device. "Latest in biometric bypasses. Should get you through any security system they throw at you."

Arthur took the device, turning it over in his calloused hands. "Impressive. But will it work on the quantum-locked systems we're likely to encounter?"

"In theory, yes," Eliza replied, a hint of uncertainty in her voice. "But we haven't had a chance to field test it under those exact conditions."

Duggins felt a familiar tension coil in his gut. Untested tech on a critical mission. Just another day at the office. "We'll make it work," he said, more to himself than to Eliza. "We have to."

As he pocketed the device, Arthur's mind drifted to the challenges ahead. The team was pushing their limits, the tech was cutting-edge but untested, and the stakes... the stakes were higher than ever.

"Anything else I should know, Doc?" he asked, his piercing gaze fixed on Eliza.

She hesitated, then nodded. "The EMP disruptors. They're... volatile. One wrong move and they could fry your own gear along with the target's."

Duggins absorbed the information, his expression betraying nothing. "Understood. We'll tread carefully."

As he turned to leave, Eliza called out, "Arthur." He paused, looking back. "Good luck out there."

He nodded, a ghost of a smile touching his lips. "Luck's got nothing to do with it, Doc. But thanks."

The training facility echoed with the rhythmic thud of fists against punching bags and the sharp clatter of gunfire from the shooting range. Arthur Duggins surveyed his team, his eyes narrowing as he assessed their progress.

Jose Beals executed a flawless takedown on a sparring partner, his movements fluid and precise. "Good form, Beals," Duggins called out. "But remember, our targets won't go down so easily."

THE EXTRACTION

Jose nodded, a thin sheen of sweat glistening on his forehead. "Roger that, sir. I'll amp it up."

Across the room, Ali Shabaab moved through a complex obstacle course, his lithe form weaving between barriers with silent efficiency. Duggins watched him closely, unable to shake the nagging doubt that tickled the back of his mind.

"Shabaab," he barked. "Let's see how you handle multiple hostiles."

Ali's eyes flickered towards Duggins, unreadable. "As you wish," he replied, his voice measured.

Duggins activated the course's advanced settings, and three holographic enemies materialized around Ali. Without hesitation, Ali sprang into action, neutralizing the threats with a series of swift, calculated moves.

"Impressive," Duggins muttered under his breath. He couldn't deny Ali's skills, but something about the man's cool demeanor set him on edge.

Suddenly, a loud bang echoed through the facility, followed by the acrid smell of smoke. Duggins spun around to see one of the EMP disruptors sparking wildly, its casing cracked open.

"Everyone down!" he shouted, diving for cover. The team reacted instantly, dropping to the floor as the device let out a high-pitched whine.

Duggins' mind raced. *If that thing goes off, we'll lose every piece of tech in here. Months of prep work, gone in an instant.*

"Beals!" he called out. "Can you reach the kill switch?"

Jose's face was a mask of concentration. "Negative, sir. It's too hot. We'd need insulated gear to get close enough."

Duggins cursed under his breath. *We don't have time for this. Every second lost is another second our enemies gain.*

"Sir," Ali's calm voice cut through the chaos. "I believe I can disable it."

Duggins hesitated, weighing the risks. *Can I trust him with this?* But as the device's whine grew louder, he knew they were out of options.

THE EXTRACTION

"Do it," he growled. "But Shabaab, if you make one wrong move–"

"I assure you," Ali interrupted, his eyes locked on Duggins', "my only interest is in completing our mission successfully."

As Ali moved towards the malfunctioning device, Duggins felt his heart hammering in his chest. This moment could make or break their entire operation. And as he watched Ali's steady hands reach for the sparking disruptor, he couldn't shake the feeling that he was about to learn just how far he could trust the enigmatic team member.

The neon glow of the diner sign flickered across Duggins' face as he slid into the corner booth. His eyes scanned the nearly empty restaurant, muscle memory from years of covert meetings kicking in. A waitress approached, but he waved her off with a polite smile.

"Coffee, black," a gravelly voice said from behind him. "Two cups."

Duggins didn't turn as the man settled into the seat opposite. "Cutting it close, Hank," he muttered.

"Traffic's a bitch, even at 2 AM," Hank replied, sliding a manila envelope across the table. "But I've got what you need."

Duggins' fingers twitched, itching to open the envelope. Instead, he locked eyes with his long-time informant. "How reliable is this intel?"

Hank's weathered face creased with a humorless smile. "Reliable enough that I'm skipping town after this. These guys don't mess around, Arthur."

The waitress returned with their coffee. Duggins waited until she was out of earshot before speaking again. "Give me the highlights."

As Hank spoke in hushed tones, Duggins felt a chill run down his spine. *This is bigger than we thought. Much bigger.*

Back at headquarters, Duggins spread the contents of the envelope across the briefing room table. His team crowded around, faces etched with a mix of determination and concern.

"Alright people, listen up," Duggins began, his voice cutting through the tension. "We've got a new wrinkle in our op. Turns out our target's got some heavy-duty backup we weren't anticipating."

He pointed to a grainy surveillance photo. "This is Viktor Kovalev. Ex-Spetsnaz, now running a private military outfit. Intel suggests he's been brought in to provide security for the handoff."

"Christ," Beals muttered. "Those guys don't play nice."

Duggins nodded grimly. "Exactly. Which means we need to adjust our strategy. Shabaab, I want you on overwatch. Your marksmanship skills might be the difference between success and a body bag."

Ali nodded, his face impassive. "Understood, sir."

"Martinez, you're our eyes and ears. I need you to hack their comms, give us real-time intel on their movements."

"On it, boss," Martinez replied, already pulling out her laptop.

As Duggins continued assigning roles, he felt a familiar tightness in his chest. *The stakes just got a hell of a lot higher*, he thought. *But if anyone can pull this off, it's this team.*

"Remember," he concluded, his gaze sweeping across the determined faces before him, "we're only as strong as our weakest link. Trust each other, watch each other's backs, and we'll all come home in one piece."

The room fell silent as Duggins finished outlining the revised plan. Tension hung in the air, thick and oppressive. Suddenly, Beals spoke up, his voice tight with barely contained frustration.

"With all due respect, sir, this is suicide," he said, eyes flashing. "We're not equipped to handle ex-Spetsnaz. We should abort and regroup."

Duggins felt a flare of irritation, but kept his expression neutral. "We don't have that luxury, Beals. The intel's time-sensitive."

"So we're just cannon fodder then?" Martinez chimed in, her usual easygoing demeanor replaced by a hard edge.

The room erupted into heated debate. Duggins watched, his jaw clenching as he struggled to maintain composure. *This is what happens when a mission goes sideways,* he thought. *The cracks start to show.*

"Enough!" Duggins barked, silencing the room. He took a deep breath, choosing his next words carefully.

"I know you're all scared. Hell, I am too," he admitted, his voice softening. "But look around you. Each person in this room has pulled off the impossible before. Together, we've faced down threats that would make most people run screaming."

He paused, meeting each team member's gaze. "We're not just some random group thrown together. We're C.O.R.E. The best of the best. And right now, we're all that stands between innocent lives and unimaginable suffering."

Duggins could see his words landing, the tension in the room shifting to something else - determination, perhaps even hope.

"I can't promise this will be easy," he continued. "But I can promise you this: I will do everything in my power to bring every single one of you home. Because you're not just my team. You're my family."

As he finished, Duggins felt a familiar resolve settle over him. Whatever came next, they'd face it together.

Arthur Duggins surveyed the room as his team performed their final equipment check. The air thrummed with tension and purpose.

"Comms check," Duggins barked, adjusting his earpiece. "Sound off."

"Beals, locked and loaded," Jose responded, his voice tight as he meticulously inspected his rifle.

Raven's cool tone cut through the air. "Blackwood, systems operational." Their fingers danced across a tablet, eyes narrowed in concentration.

Duggins nodded, satisfaction warring with anxiety in his gut. "Remember, people, we're going in dark. Every piece of gear needs to be -"

A sharp buzz interrupted him. All eyes snapped to the secure terminal in the corner of the room. Duggins strode over, his heart rate quickening.

"What the hell?" he muttered, scanning the incoming message. The screen flickered, displaying a string of seemingly random numbers and letters.

"Sir?" Jose called out, tension evident in his voice.

Duggins held up a hand, mind racing. "It's encrypted. Blackwood, get over here."

Raven glided to his side, their eyes widening slightly as they took in the message. "This isn't our standard cipher," they murmured, fingers already flying over the keyboard.

"Can you crack it?" Duggins asked, fighting to keep his voice steady.

Raven's lips tightened. "Give me a minute."

The room fell silent, save for the clacking of keys. Duggins could feel the weight of his team's stares, the unspoken question hanging in the air: What now?

After what felt like an eternity, Raven inhaled sharply. "Got it. But sir... you're not going to like this."

Duggins leaned in, reading the decrypted message. His blood ran cold. "Shit," he breathed.

"What is it?" Jose demanded, moving closer.

Duggins turned to face his team, his expression grim. "Looks like our intel was compromised. The mission parameters just changed... drastically."

Duggins ran a hand through his hair, his mind racing. "Our target knows we're coming," he said, his voice tight with tension. "And they've moved the package."

A collective gasp rippled through the room. Virginia stepped forward, her blue eyes narrowing. "How is that possible? Our intel was airtight."

"Apparently not," Duggins growled. He turned to Eli, who stood silently in the corner. "Cohen, any thoughts?"

Eli removed his sunglasses, revealing eyes filled with concern. "This reeks of an inside job. Someone tipped them off."

Jose slammed his fist on the table. "Dammit! We've been compromised. We should abort."

Duggins held up a hand. "Not yet. We still have a job to do."

"But sir," Virginia interjected, "if they know we're coming-"

"Then we change the game," Duggins interrupted. He paced the room, his mind working furiously. "We'll need to improvise. New approach, new entry point."

Ali Shabaab spoke up, his voice calm despite the tension. "I may have contacts who can provide updated intelligence. But it will come at a price."

Duggins locked eyes with him. "What kind of price?"

Before Ali could answer, the secure terminal buzzed again. Raven was already moving towards it, fingers flying over the keyboard.

"Sir," they called out, voice tight. "You need to see this."

Duggins rushed over, his heart pounding. As he read the new message, his face paled.

"What is it?" Jose demanded.

Duggins turned to his team, his expression a mix of determination and fear. "They've taken hostages. And they're demanding we deliver ourselves in exchange."

The room erupted into chaos, but Duggins' mind was already racing, trying to find a way out of this impossible situation. He knew one thing for certain: the clock was ticking, and they were running out of time.

About the Author

Brian Leslie is a Nationally Recognized Coercive Interrogation Expert, Commercial Fiction Writer and Best Selling Author. He is regularly retained by Federal, State, and Military Courts on high-profile murder cases throughout the United States.

www.thrillerbookstore.com

Read more at https://www.brianlesliemedia.com.

About the Publisher

As a boutique book publisher, we take on only a few new authors per year. We focus on building an author's brand, thereby directing more resources towards their overall success. Authors accepted by True American Publishing become creative partners, therefore, participating in their own success.